A LADY, A CHAMPION

Reporter: Are you glad you gave your life to missionary work? Don't you miss the limelight, the rush, the frenzy, the cheers, the . . . victory?

Eric Liddell: Oh well, of course it's natural for a chap to think over all that sometimes, but I'm glad I'm at the work I'm engaged in now. A fellow's life counts for far more at this than the other. Not a corruptible crown, but an incorruptible, you know.

A LADY, A CHAMPION

RUSSELL W. RAMSEY

LIVING BOOKS
Tyndale House Publishers, Inc.
Wheaton, Illinois

First printing, August 1985

Library of Congress Catalog Card Number 85–50518
ISBN 0–8423–2114–4
Copyright 1985 by Russell W. Ramsey
All rights reserved
Printed in the United States of America

CONTENTS

FOREWORD 7

INTRODUCTION 9

ONE
The Sandusky Open at Battery Park 15

TWO
A Champion for Angela's Cause 29

THREE
Angela's New Life 45

FOUR
High School, When You're Somebody 59

FIVE
Swimming with the Varsity 83

SIX
Being for Girls Everywhere 99

SEVEN
Olympic Training Camp 123

EIGHT
The XIth Olympiad 141

NINE
Angela's Crown *167*

POSTSCRIPT: MAY 1948 .... *189*

APPENDICES *195*

FOREWORD

With the conclusion of the XXIIIrd Olympiad in Los Angeles, another chapter has been written in the history of world competition. Once again athletes have shown that the spirit of competition overcomes the barrier of mores, creed, religion, and nationality.

As the youngest gold medal winner in the history of the modern Olympic Games, I feel that *A Lady, A Champion*, though fictionalized in parts, accurately tells my story of the 1936 Olympiad in Berlin. Russ Ramsey has captured the true flavor of these Olympic Games.

Angela Weber, the heroine in this story, carries the torch so many athletes have carried, going on to live a worthy, valuable life. Angela carries out the spirit of Eric Liddell's noble commitment to the "incorruptible crown" of 1 Corinthians 9:24. She demonstrates how a young girl, in her struggle to become a champion, can be her best as an athlete and a purposeful, committed woman.

I would like to share this story with you.

> Marjorie Gestring Redlick
> Olympic Champion, Three-meter Diving
> 1936 Berlin Games, XIth Olympiad

INTRODUCTION

In Berlin, at the 1936 Olympic Games, the long supremacy of the U.S. women's Olympic swimming and diving team nearly came to an end. Several of the women who stunned the swimming world in Los Angeles at the 1932 Games had turned professional. By 1936 Japan, Holland, Denmark, and Germany had developed potentially great women swimming champions.

On the third day of the finals, the U.S. women had won no medals. Then Marjorie Gestring of the Los Angeles Swim Club captured the springboard diving, leading the American women to a one-two-three medal sweep. At thirteen, Marjorie was the youngest female Olympic gold medalist in history.

The diving sweep turned the U.S. swimmers and divers around. While the Dutch later claimed to have won team honors, the scoreboard said that the U.S. swimmers and divers were the overall best. This story is dedicated to the magnificent girl who led the charge, Marjorie Gestring.

Olympic history fans may recognize that the heroine of this story, Angela Weber, is a composite of Marjorie Gestring and a Netherlands swimmer, named Dina Senff, who won the 100-meter women's backstroke at Berlin. Angela represents the glory of all the magnificent women and girls who have scaled the heights of Mount Olympus in the ancient sport of swimming.

Historical liberties have been taken in this story with the National AAU meet of 1936, and with the so-called Olympic training camp. All the Sandusky events are fictional, although the setting is completely real.

The events surrounding the 1936 Olympic Games are also real. The lives of Olympians Eric Liddell (British team, Paris Games of 1924), Glenn Cunningham (USA team, Los Angeles Games, 1932, and Berlin Games, 1936) provide an inspiring framework for Angela's fictional life, as well as her struggle to find and wear the incorruptible crown.

Gertrude Ederle (USA team, Paris Games of 1924) became a teacher of swimming for the handicapped, years after her 1926 world-record-shattering English Channel swim. Glenn Cunningham, assured of a fine career in collegiate athletic management, spent most of his life operating a farm where he and his wife, Ruth, bestowed the gift of love on homeless boys. Several of the women Olympic swimming and diving stars became teachers, nurses, swim coaches, and leaders in women's athletics. These athletes are a magnificent page in American history, and their lives serve as role models for the fictional girl named Angela Weber in this story.

Introduction

The theme of seeking the incorruptible crown comes from an interview granted by the Reverend Eric Liddell in Toronto, Canada. It demonstrates the central meaning of life for so many athletes who became champions on the running track, the playing field, or in the pool, and then wrote important moral statements upon the greater playing field of life.

This is the meaning of Angela's struggle in the present story of an American girl in the 1936 Olympic Games, *A Lady, A Champion*.

Russell W. Ramsey
August 1984

Know ye not that they which run in a race run all, but one receiveth the prize? So run, that ye may obtain. And every man that striveth for the mastery is temperate in all things. Now they do it to obtain a corruptible crown; but we an incorruptible.

1 Corinthians 9:24, 25, KJV

ONE
The Sandusky Open at Battery Park

Angela Weber's slim figure silhouetted against the bright Sandusky sky. She pressed her hands against the outside of her thighs, squared her shoulders, and riveted her eyes straight ahead.

"Weber's final dive," called the announcer, "will be the one-and-one-half gainer, pike position."

Ann Schmidt muttered to herself, "She's so far ahead already, she could fall off the board and still win."

Angela took three staccato steps down the slippery hemp matting on the diving board. With a little hop step, she arced and fired her body off the end of the board. Reaching incredible height, her body seemed to stop in midair before she dropped her head back and spread her arms wide. Suddenly she tucked her knees against her chest, keeping her lower legs straight, toes pointed. Her body spun backward toward the diving board, her head and knees missing it by two inches.

A LADY, A CHAMPION

The crowd gasped. Ann grabbed her mother's arm and held her breath.

Angela instantly opened out like a switchblade, spearing into the water vertically. Her perfectly pointed toes made only a tiny splash.

As Angela surfaced, judges began calling out her score: 9, 8, 9, 10, 10.

Only one male diver had dared to perform this dive, and he had earned a much lower score. Multiplied by the high degree of difficulty, Angela's score raced far ahead of any competition, male or female.

The Sandusky crowd quickly stood and applauded fifteen-year-old Angela for her extraordinarily daring and precise dive. The final tally put Angela twenty points ahead of the top male diver and forty-five points ahead of the closest female diver. She had broken the meet record for total points!

Three hundred spectators were thoroughly enjoying the Fifth Battery Park Open Swimming Championship. Sports booster clubs had put up medals and publicity for the big event, held in a roped-off section of the municipal harbor. Public school coaches volunteered their time to run the meet.

The final event of the 1935 meet was the 350-yard open water swim. The announcer called out instructions. "If the crowd will remain where you are, we will walk around the dock with the swimmers and you can see the finish from your present seats. The record for this event is 4 minutes, 47 seconds, set last year by John Ward of the Ohio State team."

Ann Schmidt poked her mother. "Mother, do you see what I see?" she said keeping her eyes on the activity below.

The Sandusky Open at Battery Park

"Oh, dear," said the well-dressed lady in the big sun hat. "No, don't tell me that Angela is going to compete against the boys!"

Angela walked confidently around the hot tarred surface of the Battery Park dock. With her were four boys from the Sandusky High School swim team and the two muscular mainstays of the powerful Ohio State team.

A low murmur swept through the crowd. No girl had ever competed in this event. Already, Angela's times for the 100-yard backstroke, 100- and 200-yard freestyle, and the 100-yard breaststroke were better than the times of any of the men and boys competing. Her backstroke and 200-yard freestyle times were meet records. Although she had not entered the low board diving contest, Angela's dazzling performance from the three-meter board was one that Ohio State would have liked to see from one of their men divers. And now she dared to enter the open water swim!

"I wonder," said the wealthy and influential Mrs. Dorothy Ogletree ominously, "who is taking care of that poor girl's father while she's here at Battery Park, flipping her figure around in that tight bathing outfit, embarrassing our boys!"

"Who knows?" Ann Schmidt replied. "She's late to school half the time, and she always tells the dean of girls she was fixing breakfast for her father."

"Well, does she?" asked Mrs. Schmidt.

"She says she does, Mother," Ann laughed. "But everyone knows she got paddled dozens of times last spring for being tardy. So maybe the dean of girls knows something we don't know."

Angela's friend, Mary Zimmerman, was sitting in front of the Schmidts. She whirled around. "Be quiet,

Ann, you're just jealous 'cause Angela's pretty," Mary said. "Angela has a hard life, and you ought to be proud of a girl from our own school who can come out here and beat college boys in sports."

"Sh!" Ann hissed, straining to hear the starter give the commands. They all watched one slim figure in a high-necked blue bathing suit crouch to a racing position. A few strands of Angela's long blonde hair sneaked out of the back of her white bathing cap. She leaned over, listening intently for the gun.

"Crack!" The swimmers sprang into the water. Angela and two of the larger men quickly established a lead.

Without lane markers, Angela pulled her neat, precise crawl strokes, keeping a straight course by sighting the long line of tied-up boats to her right.

Suddenly the man on her left crowded her, stealing water from her hands as she reached, and messing up her all-important high flutter kick with his big, thundering feet. As she angled slightly to the right, the swimmer on that side began to press her. Angela turned her head for a breath, and his hand pushed her face into the water. When she struggled, his hand came around again and gave her a painful blow to the solar plexus, knocking the wind out of her. At the same time, the swimmer on her left tangled his feet into hers. She began to choke, almost coming to a complete stop.

"Hey, ref, wake up!" shouted Mr. Schmidt from his seat in the bleachers. "Those two guys are interfering with the Weber girl on purpose!"

"Maybe the child will wake up and stay home next year," said Mrs. Ogletree. "A girl doesn't belong here."

"John Ward would not tolerate this," said George

Schmidt. "He's the record-holder, but he's also a gentleman. Those two fellows are trying to keep Angela from breaking his record by foul play. It's shameful."

Angela's mind struggled desperately for a way to stay in the race. Momentarily easing her stroke and slowing her kick, she perceived that the man on her left was pulling ahead. In fact, he was angling away from her, making a play to win the race. The swimmer on her right stayed on course, about two inches from her and one stroke ahead. Now, at the hundred-yard point, Angela used all the reserve strength that she normally saved for the finishing sprint. It was a terrible racing tactic, but it was her only chance. With her head buzzing and her lungs bursting, she increased the speed of her flutter kick to sprint pace and angled slightly to her left.

The bully on her right got only a glimpse of her feet passing his face. He never caught up to her again.

The swimmer on Angela's left remained half a length in front and stayed there. They both maintained a terrific pace.

Finally, Angela spotted the end of the inner harbor dock. That meant there were about seventy-five yards to go. Her body ached, but her frustration and anger shot a wave of adrenaline through her system.

The crowd went wild as Angela, in perfect form, inched past her rival, and went on to win the race by two full body lengths.

Mr. Schmidt threw his hat into the air. "This is the most incredible swimming performance I've ever seen," he said. "In fact, this town has never seen anything like it. The whole town ought to be figuring out a way to get this girl into the Olympics, and you women sit here chattering about how she ought to be at home!" he scoffed.

"Oh, Mr. Schmidt," cried Mary Zimmerman, "if only people knew how much she deserves a chance!"

"I do hope," sniffed Mrs. Ogletree, "that someone will have the decency to wrap a towel around the child while everyone stares at her."

But Mrs. Ogletree's opinion was not shared by dozens of proud Sanduskians. Wave after wave of cheers drifted over the hot Sandusky Bay sky. Finally, Angela walked up to the chief judge who sat behind a little folding table on the podium.

"Coach Miller and I compute," the chief judge announced, "that if you consider the added seconds for turns in a pool, Angela's time of 4 minutes and 32 seconds would be a new women's AAU record for the nearest comparable distances. Actually there's no way to be certain of that, but her time *is* a meet record by fifteen seconds. Had it not been for unsportsmanlike conduct by two other competitors—two men who, I hasten to add, will not be allowed in next year's competition—I see little doubt that she would have come in under four-and-one-half minutes."

The crowd cheered again as Coach Miller gave Angela a little gold medal in a cardboard box, the sixth presented to her that day.

Since Angela's only family was her invalid father at home, her well-wishers were high school friends and some of their parents. The girls hugged her excitedly, but the boys acted awkward, uncertain, even a little put off.

The Sandusky Open at Battery Park

As the crowd began to break up, Ann Schmidt called to the new Sandusky heroine.

"Oh, Angie," she yelled, "we're all going to the yacht club for dinner and a sail over to Put-in-Bay tonight. But you have your bicycle here, don't you. And I suppose you have to get home to your father. Well, congratulations!"

Angela certainly did not belong to the yacht club or the sailing club. She had nowhere to change her clothes. There was no family and no car. She threw an old skirt and blouse over her tank suit, quickly slipped into her socks and tennis shoes and stuffed her bathing cap and medals into her purse. Cramming her purse and her sopping towel into her bike basket, Angela pedaled across the hot asphalt street adjacent to Battery Park. Some people, still pulling away in their cars, waved and honked as they passed. She caught her bike tire momentarily in the old railroad tracks on Water Street, and Sandusky's swimming champion nearly fell on her face.

But with the fast reflexes of a natural athlete, Angela regained control of the bike and wearily cycled the two miles between Battery Park and the dingy wooden house where she lived with her father. There were two notes pinned to the screen door, but Angela parked her bike and hurried inside without taking the time to read them.

"That you, Angie?" called a weak voice.

"Yes, father, I'm back," she replied. It was the same ritual as always, no matter where she went.

"Could anyone get me a little coffee?" asked her father.

21

A LADY, A CHAMPION

Angela wondered if her father realized that "anyone" always ended up being her. It had always been that way. Angela's mother had died in 1920 after delivering twins. Angela's twin brother, badly damaged in the difficult birth, died three days later.

Pete Weber, Angela's father, had just taken his first job following lengthy rehabilitation after the world war. Weber had been gassed by the Germans in the Argonne Forest, and an exploding artillery round had badly damaged his intestinal system. Somehow, under heavy fire, he had dragged himself and two other men to safety.

Then there had been a Silver Star, a big story in the Sandusky paper, and marriage to his pretty nurse in the hospital. Just two years later, it all came crashing down. Weber was left with an infant baby girl, a body that functioned badly, and a crushed spirit. Veterans groups in Sandusky arranged a small pension, and a series of face-saving jobs that were mostly make-work.

Then the Great Depression hit and in 1931 Grandma Weber, who had moved in to keep house when disaster struck in 1920, passed away.

At a time when pretty little Angela, age eleven, needed a mother to teach her about becoming a woman, she became full-time maid and nurse for a father who mostly lay on the couch reading detective magazines. Angela was bright but couldn't demonstrate her ability in school. She was always tired, and there was seldom time to complete her homework assignments.

Her salvation, such as it was, seemed to lie in her persistent personality and her ability to swim and dive at a level of excellence that awed spectators.

So Angela washed clothes, hid money to pay the light

The Sandusky Open at Battery Park

bill, cooked, put up with ill-tempered outbursts from her father, and sneaked in training sessions at the junior high school pool whenever she could.

On this day, when she was the athletic queen of the city, she returned to the reality of home life by turning on the stove under the kettle. Nothing happened. Then Angela noticed that the light would not come on in the kitchen, either.

"Father, what happened to the electricity?" she asked.

"Oh, the fella came round and cut the lights off," said Pete Weber. "Maybe that coach friend of yours—David Miller—maybe he's got what it takes to make them turn the lights back on."

"Father, I gave you the money in an envelope when I rode off to Battery Park today," said Angela. "It was $8.42, enough to cover the whole month."

"Well, I needed it for somethin' else, baby," he said. "A man needs a little consolation you wouldn't understand, bein' a girl, an'—"

"You got some bum walkin' by this sidewalk to buy you a bottle of whiskey!" cried Angela. "How could you do that? I can't even run the washing machine now. And the stove won't go on!"

"Next time, stay home and take care of me, 'stead of runnin' off to Battery Park to pick up boys," said her father cruelly. "None of 'em's give you nuthin' worth havin' that I can see."

Angela kept this cruelty to herself. The idea! At Battery Park she had broken six records, beaten male college stars, showed Olympic quality in swimming and diving, and what did she have to show for it? Taunting from rich girls whose fathers had yachts and sailboats, bad sportsmanship in the water from college men who couldn't beat her fairly, and verbal abuse from her father! She knew he was working for all it was worth the sympathy he got from being a war hero and losing his wife, but now the lights were off and the stove didn't even work.

Angela stormed out of the house. Finding the notes pinned to the screen door, she plopped down on the porch to read them in the early evening light. She unfolded the first piece of paper.

> Angie,
> I got a ride over to Put-in-Bay with some of the guys. Sorry I won't see you this weekend, but you said you had to stay home with your dad again anyway. What ever happened to that Aunt Martha or someone, from Lima, that used to come help you with him? We never get to do anything anymore. I'll see you Monday if you aren't washing clothes or swimming laps.
>
> Art

So—her boyfriend, Art, was leaving her for the weekend, and she knew how, too. He was with that stuck-up Ann Schmidt and her friends on Mr. Schmidt's yacht. Some boyfriend! All they had ever done, really, was walk slowly home from school with their fingers intertwined. And there had been a couple of Saturday night movie double dates. But this was the night of her biggest athletic victory! Art was jealous—that was it—jealous of her swimming and diving. He knew that she was stuck with the hopeless drudgery of taking care of her ailing father.

Angela went to her room and peeled off her wet skirt

The Sandusky Open at Battery Park

and blouse. Stepping out of the blue tank suit loaned to her by the high school swimming coach, Angela caught a fleeting glimpse of her figure in the reflection of the windowpane before she quickly drew the faded curtains together.

Ann Schmidt was jealous too, Angela thought, *jealous because Angela was pretty, very pretty, and maybe the best girl athlete the town had ever seen.*

Mary Zimmerman was Angela's only real friend, and Coach David Miller from the high school seemed to be the only adult who took an interest in her. He risked getting into trouble by letting her use the pool at odd hours, to get her some training. Angela slipped into her underwear and a robe, then threw herself down on the bed. She squinted to read the other note in the fading light.

> Angela,
> My wife and I would like you to meet with us in the office of Pastor Bob Slayton at the Reformed Church, Monday at 9:30. You are the city's greatest athlete, and you are a fine girl. You will be glad if you come, for there are people who will help you, no matter how bad it looks for you right now. Please don't let me down.
>
> Coach D. Miller

So Coach Miller wanted the minister to counsel her! No doubt he wanted his wife there to help overcome any objections Angela might have. How could they know the pressure of having her father right in the next room, constantly calling, sometimes scolding, sometimes pleading? How could they know what it was like to be a pretty girl who owns two faded dresses, a couple skirts and blouses, cheap-looking shoes, who has to wash her underwear in the sink every night so she has some to wear the next day?

Angrily, Angela got up and went into the kitchen. Somehow, with no electricity and no hot water, she prepared a simple dinner, bathed her father, and put him to bed. Then she threw out his latest bottle of whiskey and straightened up the house.

In the humid summer night air Angela sat on the back steps, writing in her diary by the light of a neighbor's back porch lamp.

> Saturday, July 3, 1935—
> Today I won six events at the Battery Park Open. My times for the 100 backstroke and the 200 freestyle were both meet records. I stayed out of the low board in order to rest, and it paid off because I beat everyone in the high board. In the 350-yard open water, Coach Miller says my time might turn out to be AAU championship if you change it to the distances in a pool and add the turns. Two men tried to hold me out, but I got away from them. Father spent the light bill money for whiskey and now there's no electricity. Art stood me up to go over to the islands with that snooty Ann Schmidt. And Coach Miller wants to see me Monday morning in Pastor Slayton's office. I don't know why, but I guess I'll go.

Later, as Angela lay on her bed, she began to pray.

"Dear God, I thank you for staying with me in the races," she began. "I know you don't make one person win over another, but you gave me strength. And thank you for not letting me crack my head on the board, especially on the reverse dives. And help Father get

The Sandusky Open at Battery Park

better. And, dear God, is it wrong to wish that someone besides Coach Miller seemed to be on my side? Amen."

Angela fell asleep thinking of Sybil Bauer. Sybil had won the gold medal in the 100-meter backstroke at the Paris Olympics in 1924. She was fighting for girls to have access to pools, gyms, and locker rooms, and to have dignity in their sports achievements! Why, Angela wondered, did God let Sybil Bauer die of cancer at age twenty-three? Why did innocent people suffer, and good and able people sometimes go unrecognized, unsupported in their dreams?

The world was just unfair. The pastor had called it corruptible one Sunday. Corruptible. Angela dreamed of swimming between long, floating lane markers into an incorruptible world.

Although Angela didn't know it, her swimming performance had earned her the championship she needed to put her among the top three or four women swimmers in the country.

America urgently needed women swimmers and divers to challenge the rising crop of Europeans who planned to take over women's aquatic sports in Berlin the following summer.

TWO
A Champion for Angela's Cause

Angela slept until 8:30 Sunday morning, a most unusual luxury. Peeking around the window shade at the beautiful, clear day, she noticed her friend Mary Zimmerman arriving on a bicycle. Quickly, Angela pulled her robe on and went to the front door.

Mary held something behind her back. "Hi, Angie. I brought you something," she said. "You're really famous today!" With a grand flourish she produced a copy of the morning paper.

Angela pointed down the hall to her room, then put her finger to her lips, signaling Mary to avoid waking Angela's father. Angela raised the shade in her room and opened the curtains. The two girls sat down on Angela's bed to look at the newspaper.

"See? Here, page one," said Mary in a soft but excited voice. "Plus a big story on the sports page. Even photographs. And wait until those guys who tried to block you out in the open water 350 read the editorial!"

Angela pored over the articles eagerly. The front page story covered two columns bearing a bold two-line headline: Sandusky Mermaid Eclipses Men's Swim Records. The story described Angela's six victories, then continued over to the sports section, giving the entries and times for the entire meet.

"Look at the picture of you getting your sixth medal," Mary laughed. "Even that nosy Mrs. Ogletree couldn't find anything wrong with it! Angie, you look like a Hollywood swimsuit queen, even though you must have been ready to drop."

Angela's eyes sparkled and she hugged Mary impulsively. "Oh, Mary, you're the best friend I ever had," she said. "Thank you!"

Mary smiled shyly. "Angie, I brought you two papers to keep," she said.

"Oh, you remembered how Father snitched the newsboy's money to buy whiskey," said Angela with a sad little smile. "Well, a true friend is one who's there for the things you really need."

"And Angela *needs* the newspaper." Mary giggled.

The two girls read and re-read the long columns, checking the times in the little boxes following the lists of entries. Mary pulled a well-worn copy of the *Amateur Athletics Union Book of Records* from Angie's top bureau drawer, where it coexisted with Angela's Bible and a photograph of her mother. The girls talked excitedly of record times and future goals.

"What's all the commotion in there?" grumbled a familiar voice. "Can't a man get any coffee?"

Angela jumped up quickly and ran out of her room. She tapped on the other bedroom door. "Good morning, Father. It's Mary and me. Are you coming out?"

A Champion for Angela's Cause

"I'd like to come in the living room and read the paper," Mr. Weber replied, "but as I remember you sent the paper boy away."

"Put your clothes on first, then come in the living room, and I'll figure out a way to fix coffee without electricity," said Angela, trying to sound cheerful.

Returning to her room, she quickly pulled on her Sunday dress, which wasn't much different from the other one. She slipped out the back door to the neighbor's house and tapped on the screen door.

Mrs. Hudson opened the back door. "Hi, Angie," she said. "We're really proud of you, baby. I saved the paper for you. Is everything all right at home?"

"Thanks Mrs. Hudson, but no, everything isn't OK," said Angie. How she wished she didn't have to start off every conversation with a problem and a plea for help. "Thanks to Father, the electricity got turned off while I was at the open meet yesterday," she said. "There's no way to warm up coffee, breakfast, anything."

"Oh, Angie," said Mrs. Hudson, pulling the slim girl to her. "On the day of your biggest win yet, you didn't need this. Come on, I'll help you."

Quickly, Mrs. Hudson rounded up her coffeepot and some cups. As she handed Angela a basket with some rolls, she wondered how the girl could turn in great athletic performances when many times there weren't even groceries in the house.

In a very short time, Angela's motherly neighbor had organized a decent breakfast in the Weber kitchen and then left quickly. She knew that Angela's father would yell at her for "accepting charity" if he found anyone bringing in food.

After briefly thanking Mrs. Hudson, Mary and Angela

hurried to prepare a tray with coffee, rolls, an apple, and the morning paper folded open to the story about Angela. Mary followed as Angela nervously carried the tray into the shabbily furnished front room.

"Now then, Father," Angela said, mustering a pretty smile. "Look what we have here!" she said proudly.

"Ah, there's my baby," said Mr. Weber. "When you smile, you look just like your mother used to look, bringing me a tray—"

"Mr. Weber! Mr. Weber! Look at the newspaper! Angela's famous today. Aren't you proud of her?"

Pete Weber skimmed through the stories about the swimming meet, grunting from time to time. He had completely forgotten yesterday was the big day. Then something seemed to catch his attention on the editorial page.

"What's this about two bullies shoving you out of your lane?" he demanded. "Do those rich college punks think they can push my daughter around?"

The editorial lavishly praised Sandusky's sports leaders and Angela's performance, but condemned the bad sportsmanship, "uncharacteristic of this community's long record of fine athletes and fine standards both on and off the playing field."

"Oh, Mr. Weber, Angela was wonderful," said Mary, hoping to pacify his anger. "She out-maneuvered those guys and then slid right between them to beat them both. The referee barred the bullies from next year's meet."

"Hm—well, I don't suppose there's anything a sick man can do about it anyway," said Weber. "Are you girls going to church?"

A Champion for Angela's Cause

"Yes, Father. We'll leave in a little while," Angela replied. "The batteries work in the radio, so you can listen to the church service from Cleveland this morning."

Thirty minutes later, the two girls pedaled off to the 10:00 A.M. service at the First Reformed Church. Angela was eager to hear Reverend Bob Slayton's sermon and didn't even think about the small sensation her arrival would create. As Angela and Mary entered the church, two hundred worshipers surrounded Angela with kind words of encouragement and affectionate hugs. Today there were no snide comments from jealous boy athletes. There were no disparaging remarks about Angela's meager wardrobe or lack of hairstyling from girls who resented her pretty face and figure.

During the service, Pastor Bob, as the minister was known, surprised his congregation with a sermon based on his athletic accomplishments. He had been a track star in college during the 1920s and narrowly missed being on the 1924 U.S. Olympic team.

"God calls each of us," he said, "to earn and wear a crown. Sometimes it is a crown of gold, and sometimes it is a crown of thorns. But it is our life's work to make it an incorruptible crown."

Here Pastor Bob paused, and then looked directly at Angela. "In 1924, I dreamed of going to the Paris Olympics, but I failed to make the team. Now I wear the pastor's robe instead of an Olympic Medal, and I hope I am serving God as I best can."

"But there was a Scottish runner at the Paris Olympics who ran in God's name. He was Eric Liddell. His whole life was devoted to showing God's power in those who honor and serve his name. Yet Eric refused to run

33

in his best event, the 100-meter sprint, and also a relay, because the trial heats were on a Sunday. Some of us no longer honor that literal interpretation of keeping the Sabbath holy, but Eric did, and that is what is important."

The congregation listened intently, since most people preferred hearing a sports story over the expected Scripture lesson.

"God acted powerfully in Eric Liddell," continued Pastor Bob. "British officials and Scottish patriots called Eric a traitor, a religious fanatic. After all, why shouldn't even a man who ran in God's name run on Sunday? They forgot that Eric's purpose in life was to wear an incorruptible golden crown. Liddell substituted in the 400 meters and broke the Olympic record, beating the well-known American Horatio Fitch. He also took a third place in the 200 meters, behind Jackson Scholz and Charley Paddock from America. Then he returned to Scotland and spent another year in training before going to China to be a missionary, where he labors this very day.

"Three years ago, Reverend Liddell was on a rare furlough, visiting his in-laws in Toronto, and a newspaperman interviewed him. 'Any regrets about not running the 100, a certain gold medal for you?' asked the newsman. 'Regrets? Yes. Doubts? None,' Eric Liddell replied. 'And do you regret staying in China during the 1928 Amsterdam Olympics, when the 400 meters and probably a relay medal or two were certainly yours for the taking?' 'No,' said Liddell, 'no regrets or doubts there. . . . Better an incorruptible crown than a corruptible one!' "

Pastor Bob looked around slowly at his puzzled con-

A Champion for Angela's Cause

gregation. But when his glance caught Angela's eye, he knew that his sermon had hit the mark.

"Many of us," he concluded, "wear a crown of thorns. But each of us also carries a special grace, a special talent, which can free us from that crown of thorns. We strive for God's gifts to work in us, leading us to that incorruptible crown."

The service concluded with a familiar hymn, but Angela scarcely heard it. Passing through the vestibule after the service, she told Pastor Bob that she would see him the next morning at 9:30.

Many of the worshipers were puzzled by Pastor Bob's unusual sermon. Few knew anything of the burdens the young girl carried.

That afternoon, Mary helped Angela with some household chores for a while, then the two girls bicycled to Battery Park. Angela had learned that if too much time elapsed between workouts, she could get terribly stiff. Mary paddled around in the shallow water while Angela churned up and down the reserved swimming area with swift, beautiful, precise strokes.

As Angela was finishing her workout, Mrs. Schmidt drove up with a car full of teenagers. Among them were her daughter and Art Glover. They all piled out to watch Angela for a minute, and several called out sincere congratulations.

Angela pulled herself up on the end of the dock in a quick, graceful motion, whipped off her bathing cap, and shook out her long, tousled, blonde curls.

"Angela, dear," said Mrs. Schmidt, "wouldn't you be more comfortable, with all your swimming I mean, if you had some of that mop of hair cut off?"

"Mother," hissed her daughter Ann, "she doesn't

even go to the hairdresser. What would she know about hairstyling?"

Angela smiled. "I like my hair just fine, Mrs. Schmidt," she replied. "In fact, I'm going to dive without my bathing cap today."

Angela mounted the three-meter board, posed, and leaped forward into a whirling one-and-one-half somersault, her blonde mane flying in the wind. The dive was perfect.

"The nerve!" sniffed Mrs. Schmidt. "You try to give some people friendly advice. . . . Well, she has no breeding. How could she with no woman in her home and a drunken lout for a father? Come on, Ann, round up your friends, and we'll go. How would you like a special hairdo, tonight?" Mrs. Schmidt whirled on her heel and started back to the car. Ann and her friends followed.

Art Glover hung back feeling ashamed. He hoped Angela wouldn't be too angry with him. "Angie," he began, "I am proud of you. Would you like to go to the movie tomorrow night? There's a good picture playing down at the Ohio Theater."

"If you care about me, Art, where were you yesterday?" asked Angela.

"I was invited to go across to Put-in-Bay with Ann and her friends," he pleaded. "You said you couldn't go, and you know what happens to anyone who turns Ann down on an invitation. I'm from your part of town, Angie. I don't get invited out with that crowd too often."

"The point is, Art, that we are supposed to be going together," Angela argued, "but you're never there for things that are important to me. I know I'm busy a lot, taking care of Father and training. But swimming is my

A Champion for Angela's Cause

big chance. Do you want to be part of my life or not?"

"I'm ashamed of how I acted," Art said. "I do care for you. I'll just ride over on my bike tomorrow evening, OK? Fact is, that crowd of Ann's is so jealous of your looks, and your swimming, and—"

"And not one of those snooty kids has any idea what my life is like, nor cares. And I'm not sure if you do either," said Angela, plopping her purse and wet towel in her bike basket. "Come over if you want. We'll talk. I've got to make some very important decisions, and soon."

Since Art missed his ride, Angela let him ride double with her on her bike to his house. For twenty-five blocks of hard bike pedaling he felt her body against his, yet she seemed ten miles away from him!

After Mary turned off to her house, Angela rode home alone, fuming over Mrs. Schmidt's comments. Why did people have to be like that?

As Angela fixed a cold supper for herself and her father, she was genuinely unaware that some Olympic women's swimming hopefuls were being cared for by a staff of coaches, chauffeurs, maids, masseurs, and dieticians. In fact, she would have thought it was some kind of cruel joke, if anyone had told her that such amenities existed.

The next morning, with hair flying in the wind, Angela rode her bicycle to what was to become one of the most important events of her life. Dismounting in front of the First Reformed Church, she set the kickstand on her bike and entered the church uncertainly.

Pastor Bob's warm smile greeted her. "Come in, Angie. Come in," he called, ushering her into his office.

37

Angela looked around the pastor's office. Coach David Miller and his wife, Susan, welcomed her as Reverend Slayton took his place behind his desk. Across the room, an elderly lady gripping a wooden cane sat next to Coach Miller with a stack of papers on her lap. Angela took the empty chair next to her coach's wife.

Pastor Bob quickly put the girl at ease. "Angela, I don't have to tell you that Coach Miller and his wife are your most ardent supporters in carrying out your swimming training program," he said, "but I would like to introduce you to Miss Amanda Foster. Miss Foster is a friend who admires you and wants to help you with your swimming."

Angela's eyes widened in disbelief and excitement.

"Angie," said Pastor Bob, "what are you going to do with your life? You've three more years of high school, your Aunt Martha from Lima doesn't help you any more, your Grandmother Weber passed away three—no, four years ago. Your father, whom we all know you care for devotedly, is getting no better. You have little to live on. Yet Coach Miller tells me that God has invested a rare gift in you."

"I guess he means my swimming and diving," said Angela, hesitantly, "although Grannie Weber used to tell me I was pretty."

"Of course you are pretty," broke in Susan Miller. "And your swimming and diving, Angie—well, let David tell you!"

"Angie," said Coach Miller, "this has all been kind of awkward. Up until now I've bent the rules to find ways of letting you in the pool. I've tried to train you as best I could, but it's always at odd hours. Do you know that Mrs. Dorothy Ogletree called the school board to report

A Champion for Angela's Cause

that I was doing improper things with you in the locker room?"

"Oh, no!" cried Angie. "Sue, I've never done anything wrong. Why I've only been kissed by a boy once or twice. And that was in a big hurry!"

"I know, honey. It's all right," Sue reassured her. "Dave and I wish you were our own daughter. He is just telling you what he has to put up with, so you'll see what the situation is."

"The rest of the story, Angie," said Pastor Bob, "is that as of Saturday, your diving and backstroke times, possibly even your freestyle times, could get you a place on the Olympic team next summer, if—," he paused dramatically, "you trained, ate right, got enough sleep, and were relieved of the impossible burden of caring full-time for a sick parent."

"Pastor Bob," said Angela, "up until now I've only discussed these things with Sue. She's my woman friend, the only one I've had. This all so personal, but I haven't done anything wrong." Angela twisted her fingers in her lap. "I know I'm just a poor girl. The rich girls tease me constantly. Why, it took all we had to send me to Toledo on the bus last summer when I won the women's open at the YMCA-YWCA Regional Meet. I even stayed with Aunt Martha in Lima to save money. When I came back, I couldn't buy any groceries, because Father had taken what little cash we had and he—"

"Enough!" commanded Amanda Foster. "We brought this girl here to help her, and she thinks we're running this conversation like the Spanish Inquisition, because we are!" Miss Foster softened her voice. "Now Angela, dear, I've a proposition."

Angela suddenly realized who Miss Amanda Foster

was. She was the spinster who lived in the huge mansion on Wayne Street right in the middle of the millionaires' houses. Not only was she rich, but she was unbelievably wealthy.

Miss Foster interrupted Angie's thoughts. "Sixty years ago," she said, "my father sent me to school in Berlin. I learned some German, fine art and music, and the math and literature of that day. But I wanted to be an athlete, a swimmer, and a girl could not. Even a very wealthy girl, which I was, could not be a swimmer. They said it was too immodest!"

"Mrs. Ogletree always says my racing suit is too revealing," said Angela. "But Sue Miller got it for me from the high school."

"Of course, dear. It's perfectly modest. I've seen you swim," said Miss Foster. "Did you know that a Miss Etheldra Bleibtrey won three gold medals at the 1920 Antwerp Olympics? Yet just seven years ago, some people as stupid as the Ogletree woman had Bleibtrey arrested in New York City for wearing a racing bathing suit. Bleibtrey went to jail as a protest, but you won't have to," Miss Foster chuckled.

Angela relaxed, sensing she had a friend. "Are you going to get me a new bathing suit, Miss Foster?" she asked.

"Yes, Angie, and more," said Sue. "Miss Foster wants to provide the Olympic training that you deserve, all the training."

"Just as God has endowed you with swimming speed and diving grace, Angela," said Miss Foster, "so he has endowed me with lots of money and memories of a frustrated swimming career when I was a young girl. I'm quite old now, so I must soon give an accounting,

A Champion for Angela's Cause

you know. Angie, you shall be my crown, my incorruptible crown!"

Sue put her arm around Angela. "Miss Foster has hired full-time nurses to take charge of your father and the house, Angie," she said. "And she is generously augmenting David's salary, with the school board's permission to train you intensively for a year. If you can stand it, I will try to fill in as your temporary mother, or big sister if you prefer." She gave Angie a little squeeze. "You need to eat better, and you and I need to talk some girl talk. Your father will be put on pension, with a trustee to ensure that he can't squander—pardon my saying that, Angie—the money. Oh, and your weekends will include regular trips to the Cleveland Athletic Club, where you can really train. Maybe the Detroit Athletic Club, too."

Coach Miller looked at Angela with pride. "I would be honored to be your coach, Angie," he said. "The AAU championships, the nationals, are next winter, and the medal winners will essentially be the women's Olympic swim team. Angie, I think you could take a medal in the backstroke, the three-meter diving, and maybe in the 400-meter freestyle. Are you willing to try?"

Tears streamed from Angela's eyes, but she smiled gratefully. "My father, my swimming, Olympics! Oh, dear God, help me to win an incorruptible crown!" she exclaimed. "Miss Foster, God heard my prayer last night," she said in a hushed voice.

"And your tormentors will bother you no more, Angela, for you are my adopted granddaughter, the very Olympian that I wanted to be. You see," said Miss Foster, leaning forward, "Mrs. Dorothy Ogletree was turned down for membership in the Country Club this

41

year after the Board found out how her husband made his money. And the Schmidt woman—don't you know, Angie, that she failed to make the Girls' Water Ballet Team years ago at a small girls' college? And her homely little daughter—Ann, is it? The child covets your boyfriend!" Miss Foster announced. "With your assets, Angie, and me as your champion, you've neither reason nor time to bother with minor league tormentors. You're an Olympian, young lady. Now let's get started!"

Miss Foster stood and plopped a pile of business papers on Pastor Bob's desk. "These," she said, "are boring contracts that I read in my attorney's office, much to his chagrin, late Saturday evening. Let's get some nicer clothes on our swimming star and give her father the news. Then on to Berlin. We've just thirteen months to train!"

Angela was in a daze, yet well aware of what was taking place.

Sue hugged her. "Ride on home, honey," she said. "Dave and I will circle by with Pastor Bob and tell your father. Then you and I are going shopping. Before today ends," said Sue, "you will dress like the prettiest girl in town. Then we'll talk about eating, and training, and studying, and maybe even that fair-weather boyfriend of yours, Art."

By suppertime that day, Angela had a new wardrobe. The house had been fixed up to include several electric appliances. A practical nurse and a part-time housekeeper were checking in. Sue Miller had written out Angela's schedule of workouts and meets for the rest of the summer, offering her services as chauffeur. David Miller would coach her as often as it was useful, and

A Champion for Angela's Cause

when school started, Angela would receive extra help from two tutors.

To Angela's amazement, her father accepted the whole thing as if he were back in the veteran's hospital. He actually seemed pleased.

THREE
Angela's New Life

When young Art Glover rode up on his bike around 7:15 that evening, Angela was sitting on the front porch swing with her loyal friend, Mary Zimmerman.

Art would soon find out that his some-time girlfriend was no longer to be taken for granted, for Angela now had a champion fighting for her cause.

"Things are a little different tonight, Art," said Angela. "Guess I have some news to share."

Mary stood to leave. "Hey, look, you two," she said, "you need to talk things out, so I'll pedal on home. See you tomorrow, Angie."

"You're welcome to stay, Mary," said Angie. "I'm not sure that Art and I have anything to talk about. Mary, you are the friend who stood by me when I had nothing. Besides," she said with a twinkle in her eye, "you're spending the night, remember?"

"Angie, Angie, what has happened?" asked Art. "Did someone tell you something bad about me? Give me a chance; I really do care for you."

A LADY, A CHAMPION

"What's happened, Art, is that someone finally gave *me* a chance," said Angela. "It seems that two of my swimming times last Saturday, and my diving performance from the three-meter board, put me up in the top AAU rank. Maybe I'm going to make the Olympic team—maybe go to Berlin next summer—with someone to help me."

"I'll help you, Angie," said Art quickly. "I didn't know you were that good! I just thought you were kind of bitter about your family and all, and wanted to beat the guys in swimming to prove something. That's what everybody thinks, just about."

"Well, you'll all have to think again," said Angela. "Miss Amanda Foster is sponsoring me. She's hired people to care for Father. Coach Miller is going to train me—serious training. And Mrs. Miller—Sue—she's going to be my friend, like a mother to me."

"Gee, Angie, that's great, just great!" said Art. "It's like a dream, you know? Cinderella or something. But I didn't know you were so bitter. I thought you felt something for me."

"I do care for you, Art," said Angie. "But I've had to struggle hard, and you haven't been there when it was too hard for me. I don't know if I can be anybody's girl now, Art . . ." she said, her voice trailing off. "Miss Foster's offer means that I'll have to work even harder than before, but now I'll have a real chance. I can't live on swimming medals, Art, but I can show the world what God can do for a girl athlete who dares to let his power work in her. Can you understand what I'm saying?"

"Yeah, Angie," said Art, a touch of bitterness in his voice. "You're saying it's all for Angie, now. There's no room for a boy from your own neighborhood in San-

Angela's New Life

dusky. You're on your own big roller-coaster now. I just hope your car stays on the track."

Art walked down the steps and mounted his bike. Angie wondered if she should call him back. *Why should I?* she thought. *He will still be in town tomorrow. And so will a lot of other boys.*

"Angie," Mary said as Art's form disappeared down the street, "you've said I'm your best friend, the one who stuck by you when you had nothing."

"Yes, I did," said Angela.

"Well, I hope having a champion, fighting for your incorruptible crown, doesn't turn you against ordinary people," Mary warned. "I know Art has been a pill of a boyfriend, and you deserve a great guy who will treat you like a queen. But remember, Angie, take it from your best girlfriend: most of us just put one foot in front of the other and take what we can get from each day."

"You don't do that, Mary," said Angela. "You have high ideals."

"High ideals are fine, Angie," said Mary. "But remember Pastor Bob's story about Eric—Eric, who was that?"

"Eric Liddell?" prompted Angie.

"Yeah. He had high ideals," said Mary, "but as I understood the story, he gave up trying to win any more Olympic medals to spend the rest of his days preaching about God to a lot of poor people in China." She paused a moment. "Remember that thing called 'If' by Kipling in our 9th Grade Lit book last year? Something like 'And walk with kings nor lose the common touch.' Do you remember that?"

"Thanks, Mary," said Angie sheepishly. "I guess you're telling me not to get carried away, not to forget the people around me, not to turn the tables on people who were unkind to me. Thanks, Mary. You are truly my best friend."

"Do you think you'll get back together with Art?" Mary asked.

"I'll tell you a very private girl secret," said Angela. "Art is the only boy who has kissed me, and he has awful breath!"

The two girls giggled and talked for quite awhile. When the sky grew dark they went inside and turned on the radio to listen to "The Hit Parade."

The practical nurse put Angela's father to bed, and Angela enjoyed the luxury of tapping on his door, walking to his bedside like a regular fifteen-year-old daughter, and kissing his cheek.

"Good night, Father," she said. "In the morning, a lady will come to fix your breakfast. I'm leaving early to train at the Toledo YMCA. Their pool is closer to the metric distances used in the Olympics, so I can find out better how my times compare. I want you to pull for me, Father. This is my big chance."

"I know it's best this way, baby," said Pete Weber. "I've held you back far too long. Go on now and make your mother and me both proud."

Back in Angela's room the two girls talked of the future. Before long they fell sound asleep in Angela's new bed, a big bed with a real mattress that didn't sag in the middle.

Next morning, the girls awoke at 7:00 and dressed. Mary was just leaving to baby-sit for her sister when Mr. Weber's practical nurse drove up. Behind her came David and Sue Miller in their two-door Hudson sedan.

Angela felt better about leaving, knowing her father

Angela's New Life

would receive good care. During their drive to Toledo, the Millers tried to update Angela on the women who had already done well in Olympic swimming.

"Two women," said Sue, "have already won Olympic medals in both a swimming event and a diving event. David thinks we have to decide what events to prime you for, but you should be aware that you won't be the first to make it in both fields."

"Was Sybil Bauer one of them?" asked Angie.

"No, she was a great women's swimming pioneer," replied Sue. "But Aileen Riggin and Helen Wainwright are the ones I'm talking about. In 1924, Paris, Aileen Riggin took the bronze medal in the 100-meter backstroke. Sybil Bauer won the gold. But Aileen also won the gold medal in springboard diving at Antwerp in 1920, and the springboard silver medal at Paris in 1924."

Angela was still thinking about the recent changes in her life. "Did Aileen have any hard things to overcome?" she asked.

Sue laughed. "Try weighing in at seventy pounds, and measuring only four feet eight inches tall next time a couple of big bozos are pushing you out of your lane," she said.

"Gee . . ." was all Angela could say.

"Helen Wainwright took the silver in the springboard diving at Antwerp," continued Sue. "And she won the bronze medal at Paris in the 400-meter freestyle, coming in just one second ahead of Gertrude Ederle. You already know a lot about her, remember? She swam the English Channel."

"I guess I'm not the only one who's had to struggle,"

said Angie. "Isn't that what you're telling me, Sue?"

"Partly," the woman replied. "I'm also telling you that it's a tough row of corn to hoe, and there's always someone faster in the next lane."

"Coach." Angie leaned forward. "How fast do you think I'd have to swim the 100-meter backstroke to win the gold medal in Berlin?" she asked.

"Well, the reigning 100-meter champion, as you know, is glamor queen, Barbara Eastman," said Coach Miller. "She won the 1932 Los Angeles backstroke event with a time of 1:19.4. She's since brought the world record down to 1:18.2. Angie, I'd say that the woman or girl who wins the 100-meter backstroke at Berlin will have to break 1:18. Alice Bridges, up in Massachusetts, is getting close, and so are a couple of European girls. The question is whether Eastman will train seriously or not."

When they reached downtown Toledo, the Hudson glided to a stop in the YMCA parking lot. The YMCA was an imposing building with impressive facilities. Sue escorted Angie to the women's locker room. In minutes they met David at the deep end of the 25-yard pool.

"Take a thirty-lap workout, Angie. Kick ten, pull ten, and swim ten, then take a short rest. I want to put the watch on you for an estimated 100 meters."

While Angie swam the workout laps, Coach Miller asked the YMCA staff for the exact location of the metric markers. If measured exactly 9⅓ yards out from the deep end, Angie could do four laps of 25 yards each (the American Interscholastic, NCAA, and AAU distance) and then swim the fifth lap of almost 10 yards. Even then, it wasn't very scientific, because of the extra turn that would not exist in the 25-meter Olympic pool.

Angela's New Life

Allowing for that, Coach Miller had Angie train at 110 yards for the 100-meter backstroke.

As Angela was finishing up the workout, David and Sue Miller lined up two straight-backed chairs, with one edge ten yards from the deep-end wall, on each side of the pool. By sighting across while he held his stopwatch, Coach Miller could get a fairly good estimate of Angie's 100-meter time. This system would have to do until he could get her to a metric pool.

A small crowd of curious swimmers, mostly young men who worked downtown, gathered to watch Angela. She was five feet seven inches tall with slim arms and legs, a nicely developed figure, and a face that somehow stayed pretty instead of screwing up into horrid contortions like most athletes who race. Her strokes were so neat, so coordinated, so precise that without another swimmer in the water, only the knowledgeable observer realized how fast she swam.

Coach Miller recruited a volunteer, a rangy young man about nineteen years old, who said he had swum for Toledo Glass High School a couple of years before.

"I need to time the girl on 100 meters," said Miller. "Four 25-yard laps, and 10 yards back on the fifth. Would you give her a race for me?"

In spite of a chorus of catcalls from the spectators, the young man obliged, sure that he would beat the girl. He thought he could ease off near the end to keep it close, and then maybe ask her for a date afterward.

Angie rested about ten minutes after her workout; then Coach Miller cleared the pool. Both he and Sue held a stopwatch.

"Why don't you get on those backstroke starting boxes in lanes three and four," the coach called.

The big fellow hunched up about two-thirds out of the water, his face near the box. In her new shining blue racing suit, Angie's slim, feminine form looked more appropriate for a ballet than a power race.

"On your marks!" shouted Coach Miller. "Get set!" The blast of his silver whistle sent them thrashing off.

As Angie swam, she found the lane markers, a row of wooden floats strung on a tight rope, very helpful in staying on course. They also helped control the nasty little waves that always slopped over in her face when she raced against men who kicked up a bigger wake. Today her neat strokes bit little holes in the water like a pair of rotating drills. Her high flutter kick with almost rigid knees, made only a small boil. Angie's very smooth motions aptly demonstrated her knowledge of speed swimming. She was a study in economy of effort.

Angie touched the wall at the shallow end with a six-inch lead but lost it on her turn. Her legs flopped apart in an unladylike performance that resulted in a miserable pushoff for the second lap. Some of the male spectators exchanged sly grins, but the grins began to fade as Angie quickened her pace. She overtook her tall opponent steadily on the second lap. As she touched the wall, Coach Miller figured her split time for the 50 yards at 36 seconds, maybe 36.5, which for 100 yards, would be a blistering 1:12 or 1:13 in American meets! Quickly consulting a little chart with equivalent times and distances, Coach guessed that Angela might be on her way to a 100-meter time of 1:19 or 1:20.

Since Angela's persistence was always her strongest quality, she concentrated intensely on her second racing turn. Drawing her feet together tightly, just as she would do for a backward somersault or gainer off the

Angela's New Life

diving board, she dropped her head downward and fired off the wall, gaining another full yard on her opponent at the start of the third lap. She held a three-yard lead entering the third turn but then faded slightly on the final lap.

Coach Miller made a mental note to rest her a bit longer after workouts until her diet and training regimen had toughened her up a little more.

On the fourth turn, which she would not have in an Olympic pool, Angie still had a three-yard lead, and her opponent began to slow down. Angela summoned a terrific burst of speed for the final ten-yard spurt, and Coach Miller stopped his watch. The dial showed 1:20.6. The tall young man finished with a respectable 1:23.5.

Angie met her competitor at the lane divider in the middle of the pool. "Good race," she said, extending her slim hand. "Thanks for swimming with me."

"Did you swim all the laps?" he asked, huffing and blowing. "I didn't think there was anyone like you, except Barbara Eastman, maybe. Anyway, great swim!"

Angela rested for a while and then swam some freestyle laps. Several of the young men began swimming with her, and soon the YMCA pool was alive with freestylers. This made the water rough, but Angela knew that the surface condition would be like that in an Olympic race if she entered the freestyle events.

At noon she hopped out of the pool and went to the locker room with Sue.

"David has enough money to take us out to lunch, Angie, so let him do it," said Sue. She reminded Angela that she and her husband were part of Miss Amanda Foster's package contract to get her Olympian ready by

July of 1936. "After all," Sue said with a grin, "how often does a high school coach's wife get to eat lunch out in the big city?"

Angela was learning to laugh at little situations that previously had portended trouble. In the past she would worry that she couldn't afford it, she couldn't go, or someone would look down on her. Now she relaxed.

"Did you know that the diet you and Coach Miller worked out for me is about twice as much as I used to eat?" Angie said, laughing.

"You need it, Angie," answered Sue. "You are filling out, and David says you need a little more beef on you to compete with the older women swimmers. Besides, the training plan he has mapped out for you is going to burn off calories by the thousands."

When David and Sue Miller took Angela to lunch in a department store restaurant in Toledo that Tuesday noon in July, they didn't know that this was the first time Angie had ever eaten out in a real restaurant, not just a hamburger stand. Angie carefully watched Susan's moves and copied her. Angela's own natural grace, coupled with her good looks, made her seem to be doing the right thing. No one who saw Angela in her pretty yellow summer dress, chosen with exquisite taste by Susan the day before, would ever have guessed that just forty-eight hours before Angela was a girl who bore sole responsibility for an ailing parent and often didn't know where she would find food for the next meal.

After lunch, the Millers took Angela for a drive around Toledo. Angela loved the beautiful view from the bridge over the Maumee River. She bought her father a post-

Angela's New Life

card that depicted this view and put it in her purse to take home.

On the drive home, Angela talked non-stop about life with her father. Coach Miller and his wife listened, dumbfounded, to accounts of the lengths to which she had gone to feed her father, pay their bills, do her lessons, and even stay in the ninth grade at all. Somehow, she had sandwiched in swimming and diving workouts while all this was going on. Coach Miller now understood that many nights he had put her through a grueling seventy-five lap workout when she had scarcely eaten all day. The Millers kept exchanging glances as the girl poured out her feelings. They knew this all had to come out before she could move on to a new way of living and thinking.

On Wednesday, Thursday, and Friday, Coach Miller started Angela on workouts at the Battery Park swimming area. No longer was there any lack of appreciation there. In fact, the opposite was true. Now so many Sanduskians wanted to watch her or swim laps beside her that she almost preferred the old days when she swam alone.

In the afternoons, Coach Miller worked her on the diving board, but he was careful to set up the sessions for Angela's safety so that at least one diver from the high school or a college team was also there. He returned to fundamentals, taking her dives apart and forbidding her to do the elaborate ones with a high degree of difficulty. "You have a whole year to sharpen up, to tone your body, and to build your confidence," he told her.

On the first weekend after Miss Foster's proposal, Angela didn't have to train. Mary helped Angie make a scrapbook of her newspaper clippings. They also mounted all her medals on a corkboard with a frame and hung it in the Weber's living room. The girls hoped it would bring pride to Angie's father when neighbors came by.

For the rest of July and all of August, the routine was set. Angela swam laps in the morning. After a small lunch, she did her diving and then turned on the speed for sprint swimming. At least every other weekend, the Millers took her to Cleveland or Toledo to work out with some fast swimmers in a big pool.

Miss Foster rarely interfered with the program, but as Labor Day approached, she announced that they were all going to Detroit.

On Friday of Labor Day weekend, Miss Foster, Angela, Mary, and the Millers boarded the storybook-type lake steamer, *Put-in-Bay*, at the Sandusky pier and sailed across the western end of Lake Erie to Detroit. In a taxi, they toured Detroit, sightseeing and shopping as they wished.

When Mary and Angela saw the final charge on the taxi meter, they looked at each other in horror. But Miss Foster silently handed some folded money to the driver as if that was the way things were done every day.

They all watched a thrilling baseball game between the Detroit Tigers, who were in contention for the American League pennant, and the Cleveland Indians, who were not.

In the evening, they dined elegantly in a romantic dining room overlooking the Detroit River. The next day it was Angela's turn to open people's eyes. Miss Foster and Mary watched in amazement as Angela raced up and down the pool at the Detroit Athletic Club.

Angela's New Life

Coach Miller made sure that she was timed in several events.

The return trip on moonlit Lake Erie was a fantasy for Angela and Mary. Seated on the upper deck of the *Put-in-Bay,* Angela watched Susan Miller snuggled happily against David and wondered dreamily if *she* would ever meet a boy who could share her life.

The next morning Angela presented gifts to her father and sat on the foot of his bed telling him about the trip. Pete Weber watched her animated, happy face and let his mind slip back to 1919, when Angela's mother sat on his bed in the hospital and gave him the desire to recover so that he could be with her.

The following day was the first day of school at Sandusky High. Angela Weber, tenth-grader, was the tastefully-dressed athletic star—tall, slim, and radiantly beautiful. She even had her hair trimmed to shoulder length.

That first day of school Angie chose her outfit carefully. She wore a chocolate-colored sweater over a light beige skirt, and she pulled her hair back slightly with a dark brown headband.

No longer was she the poor skinny girl with the long blonde mop, who sneaked around the swimming pool at night trying to swim faster than the boys.

In homeroom, where the students checked in for fifteen minutes prior to starting their rotating schedule of six classes, Angela found out that her homeroom teacher would be none other than the dean of girls.

"Angela," said the dean, "I'll make you a deal this year."

"Yes, ma'am?" asked Angela, remembering unpleasant times in the past.

"Tell me what your problems are, especially when you break a rule, and I will help you find a solution," said the dean, smiling pleasantly.

The bell rang for the start of class, and Angela's thoughts whirled as she headed for geometry. Her father was taken care of, she had nice clothes and good food, Sue was filling in for the mother she didn't have, and David Miller was coaching her for the Olympics. Miss Amanda Foster's late-in-life wish to help a girl become the swimming champion she couldn't be made the difference.

Somehow, Angela thought, there was supposed to be a boy, or better said, a boyfriend, with whom she could share her exciting new life.

FOUR
High School, When You're Somebody

During the first class, Angela decided she was going to like geometry. It was neat and logical, and if you put the lines and angles where they were supposed to go, it all came out just right.

The teacher was a quiet but firm little man who kept the class on task. He also used examples from jobs, sports, and home life to explain the theorems that sometimes made geometry frightening to students.

The minutes zipped by, the week's homework assignments were given out, and the bell rang for the end of first period. Angela gathered her books and started toward the door. Moving into the crowded hallway behind her friend Mary Zimmerman, she felt someone catch her by the arm.

"Say, where have you been?" said a pleasant male voice.

Angela looked up into the smiling, handsome face of

Ted Gunter, the star quarterback of the Sandusky "Blue Streaks" football team. Ted's navy cardigan letter sweater proudly displayed a huge navy-colored "S" with white piping, adorned with a football, a basketball, and a track shoe.

"I heard there was a new athlete in the locker room," Ted laughed. "I've been hoping for a chance to get to know her better."

Angie's heart pounded. "Oh, hi Ted. Sure," she said, suddenly aware that all eyes were on the two of them. "I have English class next period. Do you want to walk toward the old building with Mary and me?"

In no time, Sandusky High School's two top athletes were swapping information about training schedules, coaches' rules, and about trying to find time and energy to study when they were tired at night. Mary walked beside her friend in silence, happy to see Angela's new popularity.

As the two athletes talked, Angie couldn't help but stare at Ted's letter sweater. The combination of blue stars and stripes on the sleeve indicated Ted had earned six varsity letters: two each in football, basketball, and track.

When they reached the old building, Ted grinned down at her. "Well, here's your class," he said. "Look, I've got football practice this afternoon at four o'clock out at Strobel Field, but I'd like to call you this evening, say around 7:30?"

Angela nodded. "I hope football practice goes well for you. I'll think about you, running plays at Strobel Field while I'm swimming laps at the junior high pool."

"Thanks. I'll talk to you tonight," Ted said, moving on to his next class.

High School, When You're Somebody

Angela silently thanked Miss Amanda Foster for providing them with a telephone. Fortunately Susan Miller had coached Angela a little in the sport of romance so that she wouldn't blurt out such things as, "Oh, yeah, we finally have a phone now." Ted lived in one of the best neighborhoods in Sandusky and no doubt knew all about Angela's new financial situation, but there was no need to announce it.

Just then Ann Schmidt walked up behind Angela. "Looks like certain people are moving up," she said with a little grin.

"Yes, Ann," said Mary Zimmerman. "And Ted is one boyfriend you won't steal with your father's boat. Ted's father has a bigger boat than you do!"

There was a round of laughter among the girls who were entering Miss Lois Hartung's tenth grade English class. Angela sat down at a table for six, directly across from Mary.

"Welcome back, class," said Miss Hartung. "You all know what we do on the first day of my English class. You have fifty minutes to write a theme entitled 'What Affected Me the Most This Summer.' You will turn it in before you leave. Neat writing, please, or you will take an 'F' and do the theme over at home. There is a dictionary on each table."

Miss Hartung walked quietly around the room as the students wrote. Stopping behind Angela, she leaned over the girl's shoulder.

"I know you have a lot to tell about, Angela, but you do not have to write anything too personal," she said in a low voice. "And I want you to see me after third period. I will take you to lunch today so we can plan your tutoring sessions. Your schedule is so occupied that we must make the best use of the time you have.

"Yes, Miss Hartung," whispered Angela. "And thank you."

Angela had no trouble telling how her big wins in the Battery Park Open had gained her a champion for her cause and thereby changed her life. What was hard was telling what it meant to her. She was thankful that writing came fairly easily. Maybe it was due to writing in her diary every night, a practice she had persistently observed since she had learned to print.

In her third class, biology, Angela found that she would have to memorize a lot of new words.

And as many times as she had gone swimming in Sandusky Bay, she didn't know that a former Sandusky High School teacher, Professor Edwin Moseley, had done famous work in collecting specimens of the creatures that lived in and around that water. Why, her father must have been in Mr. Moseley's class, maybe in this very room! I'll have to ask him, she thought.

When biology class ended, Angela returned to Miss Hartung's room. Miss Hartung picked up her purse and led Angie out by a side door. After a short walk through the park, she unlocked the door to her apartment in an old limestone house three blocks from school.

Over a simple lunch, Miss Hartung discussed her plan with Angela. She had already made tutoring arrangements with Mr. Thomas, Angela's geometry teacher. Each Saturday morning, Angela would have a two-hour tutoring session with Mr. Thomas, who lived a few blocks from Angela's. Then she would ride her bike to Miss Hartung's apartment for lessons in English and writing.

High School, When You're Somebody

"How much time will you have for studying at night, Angela?" asked Miss Hartung.

"As much time as the other students, Miss Hartung," said Angela. "Coach Miller had my schedule set up so I have study hall during the sixth period. Instead of studying, I walk over to Jackson Street to work out in the junior high pool. I can train until 5:00 P.M., when they close the pool for dinner."

"What happens in December, Angela, when the boys on the high school swimming team start practicing over there?" asked Miss Hartung. "They don't wear bathing suits, and even if they did, I don't think you'd feel comfortable, being the only girl in there."

"Oh, Coach Miller is very strict about what I can do around the boys' swimming team," said Angela. "I have to clear out of the pool at four when they start practices. They have time trials on Fridays, and since Sue, Coach Miller's wife, comes they always wear their suits. I'm going to race the boys each Friday. I'll have dinner at home with Father each night, and I'll have two hours to do my homework. The chlorine they use in the pool water makes my eyes sting and makes me feel sleepy. But I made it last year, working out evenings in secret. Things are so much better now."

"I just hope," said Miss Hartung gravely, "that you have time to be a girl. I admire the brave way you used to live. And I applaud your noble goals, especially what you said in your theme about earning an incorruptible crown. So many athletes just win the medals and the trophies, and then have nowhere to go."

After lunch, Angela helped Miss Hartung quickly wash the dishes before they returned to school.

A LADY, A CHAMPION

"Thank you for your advice, Miss Hartung," said Angela as they parted. "I'll see you in class tomorrow, and I'll be at your house on Saturday, ready to work."

In the afternoon, Angela had World History and Latin II. Angie's Latin teacher, an older woman, asked her the correct Latin word for a building with a swimming pool. Angela stammered, "a nata—nata—natatorium."

The class laughed, but the Latin teacher then amazed the students with stories of Roman women using the beaches and swimming in the Mediterranean centuries before anyone argued over the women's place in team athletics.

As the bell rang to end the fifth period, the Latin teacher, who was rumored to have known Julius Caesar personally, wrote on her blackboard in yellow chalk: *Angelia—Natare Est Vincere.*

Angela blushed. "Thank you, ma'am," she said, leaving quickly for swimming practice. Hurrying to her locker, Angela smiled to herself. *Sandusky High School is a pretty nice place to be*, she thought, *when you're somebody!*

Seven blocks away, at the junior high, was Sandusky's only indoor pool. As Angela hurried into the girls' locker room, she heard an eighth-grade girl whisper to her friends who were getting dressed. "It's her, Angela Weber!" Several girls stared.

Angela could not pass by without notice. "Hi," she said. "I'm Angie. You're welcome to swim laps with me if your coach will let you."

"Oh, no—" said one girl, "but could some of us watch?"

"Sure," Angie replied, "but it gets real boring. You'll see!"

High School, When You're Somebody

The girls stared, though not meaning to be rude, as Angela peeled off her skirt and blouse. Maybe, she thought, they wondered if her body was like that of some creature from another planet. Angie tried to be nice to the awed younger girls. After all, wasn't she struggling for girls everywhere to have the right to be athletes? Wasn't that part of her incorruptible crown? So Angela did not ask the younger girls to leave, but turned modestly as she changed into her blue racing suit.

Quickly Angie locked up her purse, snatched her towel, and happily headed for the pool. This was her element. This was where she was queen.

But Coach had evidently forgotten she was a queen, for he had left a very abrupt note on the blackboard:

> Angela—Kick 20 laps freestyle, 20 backstroke. Pull 20 freestyle with your feet rubberbanded to the kickboard and quit jerking your rear end up on the end of each stroke. I'll be here at 4:30. Coach.

Angela's cheeks flushed a little as she read the note, but she did the workout and felt strong. Coach Miller came in as she was finishing.

"I want to time you on a 400-meter freestyle today," he said. "We still haven't decided on all your events, but that's a good one for building up racing endurance. And," he added, "for keeping your whole body smoothly in line, not jerking."

The 400 meters converted to a 440-yard swim, which was 22 laps of the junior high's 20-yard pool. Angela put all she had into it and registered a 5:38 time.

"You look good, Angie," said Coach Miller. "I know

you're tired. How was your first day of school?"

"Fine. Very fine," said Angela. "My tutors, Miss Hartung and Mr. Thomas, are all set up for Saturday morning. And Coach, don't tease me, but this is important to me—"

"OK, honey, what is it?" he asked.

"Ted Gunter's going to call me at home tonight," Angela said with a twinkle in her eye. "I think maybe he's going to ask me out on Saturday night. Oh, please tell Sue!"

"I will, Angie." said Coach Miller. "And Ted Gunter's welcome to ride along with us Saturday afternoon to the Rocky River High School Natatorium. There, a certain Olympic hopeful will be training Saturday evening and all day Sunday on the three-meter springboard, since we only have a one-meter board here."

"Oh, Coach—," said Angela, crestfallen.

"I'm sorry, Angie. I do understand. You looked like a dream in your new outfit today. I saw you in the hall, earlier," said Coach Miller. "But Ted Gunter is a three-sport, year-around varsity athlete, a true star," he continued. "And Ted, of all people, knows the price of athletic excellence. You need this training."

The custodian came in with his big ring of keys, indicating that he wanted to have dinner before he had to be back for municipal open swimming in the evening.

"OK, Coach. I'll do what you and Sue tell me to do," replied Angela. "Are there any dreams that don't have ugly little bricks attached that fall on your head?"

"None," said Coach. "Lock that girls' locker room door behind you. Call Sue at home tonight if you want, and give my regards to your father."

High School, When You're Somebody

At 5:45 Angela and her father sat down to a nice dinner which the housekeeper had prepared for them. Angie tried to fix herself up so that she didn't look bedraggled. She didn't want her father to feel that he was being pushed out of her complicated new life.

"Did you have a nice day, Father?" she asked brightly.

"Oh, fair-to-middling," he said. "That morning lady who comes here, she's a pip!"

"How is she a pip?" asked Angela, hoping her father hadn't said something dreadful to the highly proper practical nurse.

"A real drill sergeant, you know? Like when I signed up for the Great War and went down south on a train. This big sergeant, he scared you more than the Germans! And she's like that. 'No smokin' in bed, Mr. Weber!' she yells. 'Put them slippers back on. You'll get splinters in your feet!'"

"Sounds like the way Coach Miller keeps after me," said Angela, ruefully. "He's my drill sergeant. 'Twenty more laps, Angie!' and 'Keep your rear end down, Angie,' and lots more."

"You're the champ, honey, and prettier every day," said Peter Weber. "Was high school OK today?"

For a moment Angela blinked back tears. She had never known her father to remember her birthday, her swimming meets, or her first day of school.

"I started biology today," she said. "They have cases and cases of fish, birds, bugs, and all kinds of things collected by a Professor Edwin Moseley. Was he your teacher in high school?"

"He retired a little before my time," her father replied. "Fact is, in 1916 I think it was, not long before I dropped out to join the army, I got a licking from the principal. Fooling around in the biology lab, us boys were, and someone gave me a hard shove, and I broke a glass panel on Professor Moseley's collection."

Angela laughed in delight. This was the happiest dinner with her father that she could remember. Maybe, she thought, just maybe Father would get better, and things would be more normal as her ability grew and as she got older.

From long habit, Angela cleared and washed the dishes.

"Father," she said, "I'm expecting a call from a really nice boy, Ted Gunter. Please be sweet if you answer. For me, please?"

"He must be something, Angie," said her father. "Old man Gunter, he's a big shot in the paper box factory. OK, baby, I'll be nice."

Just a few minutes after Angela spread her books on the kitchen table and started writing out the answers to her geometry exercises, the phone rang. Her Father, true to his word, answered pleasantly, handed the phone to her, and shuffled off with his cane to his bedroom.

"Hi, Ted," said Angie, anxiously.

"Hi, Angie," Ted replied.

They chatted about high school friends and about their training, then Ted asked the anticipated question.

"Could I pick you up Saturday for a party at our house, Angie?" asked Ted. "Just four couples."

Reluctantly, Angela told him about her weekend schedule of tutoring Saturday morning, then the drive to Cleveland with Coach Miller and Sue, a springboard diving workout Saturday night and all day Sunday, then

High School, When You're Somebody

home late Sunday night. "I really would like to go out with you, Ted," she apologized. "I hope you understand. I know you have a high commitment to athletics."

"Why sure. The real question is, can you make *any* time in your schedule for me?"

Deeply relieved, Angela suggested a plan. "I have no workout on Friday. Coach said something about backflushing the pool filter. Suppose I rode my bike out to Strobel Field and watched you at football practice?"

"Suppose I pick you up and take you to practice in my Ford coupe," countered Ted. "You get out at 3:00 like the football guys do. Why don't you ride your bike straight home, and I'll follow you. Then I'll drive you out to Strobel. By the way, I've got an extra ticket for you to see the opening game against Lorain a week from Friday night. I hope you'll sit with Mother and Dad."

"This Friday is fine, Ted," said Angie, "but I'll have to check with Coach Miller about next week. Thanks."

"Great. See you tomorrow," he replied.

When Angela finished her homework around 9:30 that night, she had a feeling that maybe she had found the right boy.

Throughout the first week of school, when Angela would see Ted in the hallway, they would talk briefly and the school was buzzing with tales of a storybook romance.

On Friday Angela selected a white pleated skirt and a green blouse, and a matching hairband.

Ted walked Angela to English class, where the students were deeply into Shakespeare's *Romeo and Juliet*. On the blackboard, some wit had scrawled, "Tomorrow's Assignment: 'Tedeo and Angeliet' by Shakespeare, Act V." Several students turned to Angela and snickered as various students read the romantic passages.

Miss Hartung pretended not to notice, but led the students into the tragic part of the play. As they approached the great scene of Juliet's lament, she steered the reading to Angela's table. As Mary read aloud, the class stopped giggling and discovered why Shakespeare was still being studied in 1935.

"Well done, Mary. You've obviously prepared today's lesson," said Miss Hartung. "Angela, continue, please."

Angela's eyes had strayed ahead, and something ominous flashed in her mind. She quickly returned to the present and found her line to read.

"When I shall die," read Angela, stumbling at first, "when I shall die, take him and cut him out in little stars; and he shall make the face of Heaven so fine, that all the world will be in love with night, and pay no worship to the garish sun."

"And what did Shakespeare mean here, Angela?" asked Miss Hartung. "Is Juliet saying that her lover is better off dead, lighting up the face of heaven?"

"No, no, ma'am," said Angela, "she's saying—" Angela's eyes misted over. "She is saying that his life was a treasure, and that in death, the treasure of his life lighted up the darkness. She's saying that his life," Angela's voice became a whisper, "was his incorruptible crown."

"Hmm, an incorruptible crown," repeated Miss Hartung. "That's profound, Angela, and very moving. Let's read on."

Mary and a few students who knew more about An-

High School, When You're Somebody

gela's life understood the chord that had been struck as Angela read, but most of the class thought that Angela was just acting soupy over her new boyfriend.

At 3:00 Angela hurried home, dumped her books, and ran out to get in Ted's coupe. On the drive down Hayes Avenue to Strobel Field, Ted apologized for the smells inside his car. "Hauling around football players in season," he pointed out, "makes your car smell of tape, wintergreen, leather, and sweat."

Angela giggled.

"Not many girls watch the practices, Angie. I hope you won't mind being left alone with the cheerleaders," Ted laughed. "I'm not sure how they'll act. Ann Schmidt is on the squad."

As the players ran their warm-up drills, Angela walked along the sidelines. Then an intra-squad scrimmage began, and one of the assistant coaches offered Angela a seat on the empty bench. Angie sat down, pulling her white skirt tightly around her knees.

"Repeating S!" shouted the cheerleader captain, sending the blue-and-white outfitted girls into a cheer routine. Angela watched them do leaps and splits, while their little blue skirts bounced and whirled and their hair bobbed up and down.

When the routine ended, Angela walked over to talk to the girls. She wanted Ted's friends to be her friends, and Sue Miller had advised her that making friends with the cheerleaders would prevent a lot of jealous talk behind her back. "Hi, Angie," said Marsha Glen, the captain. "Did Coach Miller let you off today?"

"Yeah, pool cleaning or something," said Angela. "Your routine looks great. I know the players love it."

"Why don't you do the next one with us, Angela?" said

Ann Schmidt. "It's our somersault. You know, the one where pairs of girls form a four-hand bridge and flip each other over. With great diving ability, it should be easy."

"Well . . . well I . . . I'm wearing my skirt," Angela stammered. "I'd be glad to work out with you if I could borrow some shorts."

"You're welcome to work out with us anytime, Angie," cut in Marsha quickly. "You could teach all of us how to improve flips. But I doubt if Coach Miller leaves you any free time."

"She could do it right now, Marsha," said Ann. "She doesn't get embarrassed about what shows when she dives in front of a big crowd, do you Angie?"

"Pipe down, Schmidt," Marsha rebuked. "We're wearing blue shorts that match our skirts. Angela's competition swimsuit is cut exactly the same way as our shorts, and you know it."

"Take a shower, Schmidt," cut in another girl. "Angie is the best athlete in our school, boy or girl, and our job is to cheer our athletes on!"

Angela was pleased that the other girls were sticking up for her, but she knew that Ann Schmidt would just wait for the next opportunity to humiliate her. Waving amiably, Angie resumed her seat on the bench and concentrated on the football action, hoping to remember some details to discuss with Ted. She kept hearing the coaches yell about stance and about firing off the crouch position, so she studied these motions intently.

When the scrimmage ended, all the players ran five laps around the track. Tired and out of breath, Ted passed by Angela en route to the locker room.

"Give me fifteen minutes, and I'll drive you home,"

High School, When You're Somebody

he grunted, running off the field with a row of sweaty football players.

As they drove home, dusk was falling, the soft smell of burning leaves filled the air and a hint of cold wind was blowing south off Lake Erie. Quickly, Angela tried to show Ted another athlete's perspective on what she saw at practice. She hoped he would enjoy a girl who was interested in "firing off a three-point stance."

He did. "Will you be with my parents at the Lorain game here next Friday?" he asked hopefully.

"Yes, Coach says I have to work out, but I'll rush home and fix myself up so your parents will be proud of me," said Angela.

When they reached Angela's house, Ted noticed her movements as she got out of the car. There was grace, discipline, and the athlete's economy of motion in every move. *She isn't just pretty,* Ted thought. *She's classy, sort of a home-grown aristocrat!*

The next day, Angela studied hard at both tutoring sessions and then left for Cleveland with the Millers. At the Rocky River High School pool, Coach Miller put her through a grueling session on diving fundamentals. By the end of four hours, all three of them felt tired and grouchy.

Again on Sunday, after they attended an early church service, they put in six hours of diving practice. Coach Miller felt that Angela had developed too fast and that there were technique errors in her tough repertoire. Angela was defensive about the risks she was willing to take, such as shaving the board closely on the inward dives. She wondered why Coach Miller couldn't understand that she had learned her three-meter springboard routine in bits and pieces with very little coaching. Over and over, Sue Miller made peace between her husband and his protégeé.

On the way home, the Millers reviewed Angela's first week of school and decided that things were going well. Although her coach was tough with her, Angie was grateful that both he and Sue cared so much.

The second week of school flew past with the same schedule, and soon it was the night of the opening football game. Angela rushed home and changed into a gray plaid wool skirt and navy cable stitch sweater. Since the night would turn colder, she got out her tan topcoat and a bandana. Angie was surprised when the doorbell rang.

"Hello, I'm Al Gunter, Ted's father. I'm so glad to meet you, Angela," said a handsome man in a business suit.

"Mr. Gunter, hello. I didn't know you were coming to get me," said Angela. "This is my father, Mr. Weber. Father, this is Mr. Gunter."

"Nice to meet you," said Pete Weber, hobbling on his cane to greet their visitor. "Come in, come in if you want to."

Mr. Gunter was a gentleman, and he put people at ease, making them quickly forget that he was a senior company executive with enormous responsibilities.

"We're so proud of Angela, Mr. Weber," said Ted's father. "Everywhere I go people are talking about how she has finally given Sandusky an Olympic hopeful. I know it can be tough having a young athlete around the house."

Mr. Weber was relieved that Gunter talked to him like an equal. They chatted pleasantly about football, Sandusky High School, and some new construction in

High School, When You're Somebody

town. After a few minutes, Angela went to the door with her coat and cleared her throat.

"We'd best be off," said Mr. Gunter. "My wife will have dinner waiting, and Ted leaves early for the stadium on game nights. He'll have Angela home before midnight. You have my word on it, Weber."

As Angela rode with Ted's father in the gleaming twelve-cylinder Packard, she tried to remember the etiquette Sue had taught her. When they arrived, Mrs. Gunter welcomed Angela with delight, although Ted was just leaving for the stadium.

"I know you'll play a great game, Ted," said Angela. "I'll be cheering for you."

"Thanks," Ted replied. "You see, Mother, Angela doesn't giggle and say, 'Good luck, Ted,' like certain other girls do. She's an athlete too, and she knows you make your own luck."

"Yes, Ted," said Mrs. Gunter, "but I think Angela would agree that God watches over you, too."

"Oh yes, Mrs. Gunter," said Angela. "Everything you do on the field, in the pool, all athletics—it's God's power working in you."

"Well, do your best, son," said Mr. Gunter. "We're going to enjoy Angela's company for dinner, and then we'll all be cheering for you at the game."

Their candlelight dinner was simple but delicious. Angela felt comfortable with the Gunters. She kept wondering if life might have been like this in her family if her mother had lived. She directed the conversation toward Ted's achievements, not wanting the Gunters to think her vain or self-centered.

During the football game, the Gunters treated Angela like a daughter. Together they watched intently as the

75

game remained tied 7-7 from early in the first quarter. The fierce Sandusky-Lorain rivalry had never been stronger.

Ted kept his team together, watching for a chance, and saw a weakness off right tackle. An oversized defensive lineman was charging regularly through his smaller Sandusky opponent, but he started each play from a high crouch. Remembering Angela's observations after practice about firing off the crouch from a perfect body position, Ted keyed up a special play with forty-five seconds left in the game, and Sandusky in possession at midfield.

Changing the usual numbers for an off-tackle series, Ted sent the Sandusky right tackle firing through on an unexpected call, hitting the high-crouched lineman at ankle level. Down he went as Ted faked the halfback handoff, then high-stepped through the hole where there had been a charging express train all night. Ted broke quickly through and charged for the sidelines, with one tackler left to beat.

Just as the last defender was about to shove Ted out of bounds on the fifteen-yard line, Sandusky's other halfback raced up and took a low-scooped lateral, sprinting over the goal line as the crowd went wild. Lorain got off two courageous plays that gained long yardage, but it was not enough. The Blue Streaks had won a 14-7 thriller.

Later, Angela and Ted drove to a party for football players, their dates, and the cheerleaders. The party was fun but boisterous.

"Would you like to drive around for a while with me, Angie?" asked Ted.

High School, When You're Somebody

"I would, Ted," replied Angie, "as long as I'm home by midnight."

After taking a roundabout route, Ted's Ford coupe pulled into Battery Park, the scene of some of Angela's biggest swimming triumphs. Ted cut the engine, and the two of them watched the moonlight shimmering over Sandusky Bay. A chilly autumn wind blew, and Ted rolled up the windows.

For half an hour they talked. Ted talked about college the following year, then medical school around 1940. Angela shared her dreams for the Olympic Games in Berlin, but said she could not visualize what she might be doing by 1940. They both agreed that they could not live on athletic achievements, but that sports were a vehicle to a bigger life. They laughed together about nosy Sanduskians who had their eyes on a possible romance between the two great athletes.

Angela looked at her watch and saw midnight fast approaching.

"Ted, I have to go home soon," she said. "You played beautiful football tonight."

"Angela, for an hour I've been wanting to ask if I could kiss you, but everyone said you didn't—er, wouldn't," Ted stammered.

"And the girls have been saying that you can kiss anyone you want, and that I'd better be ready," Angela laughed. "One thing is sure. It's a sport where I haven't had much training!"

"Well, I respect you, and I care for you, I—"

"You were wonderful tonight, Ted, and I care for you, too," said Angie.

As the moon gleamed on the hood of the little Ford,

Ted slipped his arm around Angela and drew her to him. Their lips met briefly, and then Angela relaxed in Ted's arms, feeling secure against his firm, muscular chest. "I have a lot to learn about this," she said. "I know there are plenty of girls who won't insist on going home by midnight, but. . . ."

"But they won't have your treasures, Angie," said Ted. "You are a girl of great quality. Mother spotted it before I even met you."

After Ted took her home Angie found herself singing as she hung up her clothes. Tomorrow there would be tutoring, and swimming every afternoon, and studying most nights. This weekend it was diving at Toledo—no, she forgot where—but it would all be different now. Ted cared for her. She would try to be his girl, even if her time was limited and her personal standard high. Perhaps, as Ted said, her high standards were what attracted him to her.

As autumn claimed Sandusky, Angela settled into her strict routine. She found a great deal of security in her father's support, Sue's motherly love, and Coach Miller's stern discipline. With weekly tutoring her grades improved markedly. Mary Zimmerman remained Angie's touchstone, providing loyal friendship and a link with her past.

And bright, pretty Angela had earned the attention of Sandusky's star football player. As their relationship grew, Sue Miller warned Angie that many girls find little substance in such attractions, and some get burned. Angela wasn't worried. Committed to not compromising her personal standards, Angie felt that she and Ted had a chance for genuine love.

In November, their relationship faced a crisis. Coach

High School, When You're Somebody

Miller insisted that Angela participate in an important open meet at the Detroit Athletic Club on the same night as Sandusky's homecoming football game against powerhouse Elyria. The young couple would be unable to support each other at these important milestone events in each of their careers.

Angie watched a couple of football scrimmages, and Ted tried to look interested while Angie swam laps and time trials, but it wasn't the same as being there to cheer each other to victory.

On Thursday of the week before Thanksgiving, Angie left for Detroit with the Millers.

At the meet Friday, Angela faced regional and national swimming stars. After winning first place in the 100-yard backstroke, the 200-yard freestyle, and the three-meter diving, she took second in the 100-yard freestyle and third in the 100-yard breaststroke, an entry which Coach Miller decided to forego in the future.

Back home, Ted led Sandusky to a thrilling one-point homecoming victory. Ann Schmidt spent the entire homecoming ball trying to get various pretty girls and former girlfriends of Ted's to dance with him, so that Angela would get bad news upon her return.

Saturday night, the young couple went to a party and then drove around to the Bay Bridge and Marblehead Peninsula. Watching the cold swells out on the open water of Lake Erie, they talked.

"I got a lot of gossip about you," Angela said, laughing. "Just to show you I don't believe it, I'll snuggle against you."

She leaned against Ted's chest, lay her cheek on his shoulder and drew her legs up on the seat beside her.

"How do I know you didn't have a big time with one

A LADY, A CHAMPION

of those international swimming stars up in Detroit?" asked Ted. "You, madam, have a lot to offer any man."

"First," said Angela, "the ones I met are all full of themselves—standings, their press releases, and their next invitational meets. Second, I was with the Millers every minute. Third, I care for you, Ted, and I choose to be your girl."

Ted smiled down at her and the two of them stared silently out over Lake Erie. After several minutes Ted spoke. "Mother said you would be welcome for Thanksgiving dinner. You can bring your father if you want," he said. "She wants to make it comfortable for you. We can send dinner to your father at home if you'd prefer."

"Your mother is so sweet to me," said Angie. "I hope I won't let you down. I know you've been lots of places and learned lots of things that I haven't done. When you met me, my life was changing a lot."

"Angie, if you're thinking that we're snobs, or that we look down on you because you don't have as much money, that's just not so. Dad says," Ted added ruefully, "that you're the first real lady I've ever gone out with. He says you make me behave."

"Maybe I do, Ted." She laughed. "It's time to go home, but first. . . ." Angela turned toward him. And they kissed tenderly. After several moments, she moved over on the seat and smiled. "Thanks for not pushing me. I really feel I can trust you."

Ted gave her a little squeeze but didn't reply.

"Congratulations, by the way, on a terrific football game while I was gone," Angie said. "I don't know how you got along without my little coaching tips. Think what we could do on the same team!"

Ted chuckled and kissed her hair impulsively.

High School, When You're Somebody

"You're the greatest. When the varsity swimming season starts in January, I'm going to support you like nothing you've ever seen," he said. Cranking up the Ford coupe, he pulled Angie closer, and with her head on his shoulder, he drove his girl home.

FIVE
Swimming with the Varsity

Angela had a quiet Thanksgiving dinner with her father, after graciously declining Mrs. Gunter's offer. In the evening, Mary Zimmerman came over and they mounted Angela's newest medals in the growing collection on the living room display board.

On Friday, since there was no school, Angela had a long workout at the junior high pool. Angela was just starting her laps when the door from the girls' dressing room opened and Marcia Glen, captain of the cheerleading squad, walked over to the side of the pool. Then from the boys' side came Coach Miller with Ted Gunter.

Angela seldom stopped a workout, but this looked like something important. She pulled in at the deep end and did her appealing little kick-pull-and-twist exit from the pool.

"Hi, Angie. I have a little surprise for you today," said Ted.

"Hi, Ted. Marcia. Thanks for coming over," said Angela.

"As varsity swimming coach," said Coach Miller, "I'm used to getting by on very little. We don't usually get the money and the support that the major sports get. But that was before you and Ted opened up some doors."

"Angie," Marcia picked up the story. "Next month we start working on our routines for the basketball season," she explained. "Ted is incoming basketball captain, as you know, and he asked me if the swimming team could get some support from the cheerleading squad."

Coach Miller continued. "Angie," he said, "Ted and Marcia have talked to Bill Wilkie, the incoming swimming team captain, and—"

"We're going to have cheerleaders at all the home swimming meets, Angie," said Marcia excitedly. "We'll even try to have a couple girls at your practices, since the pool is right downstairs from the basketball gym. That way, there'll be some girls to keep you company."

"See what a good influence you have on everyone, Angie?" said Coach Miller. "You're helping the whole swimming program here. Now," he said abruptly, "I thought I'd let Marcia and Ted time you today on some sprints. There's a list on the board."

Angie basked in all the attention. She finished her laps, hoping the others wouldn't get bored, and then put her absolute best into her timed sprints. Ted gave Angie her starts with coach's silver whistle, while Marcia operated the round silver stopwatch on a red cord.

As Angie came steaming into the finish, Marcia tried to be ladylike while squatting down to see Angie's hand

Swimming with the Varsity

touch the wall. She almost fell in! And by the time Angie finished, Marcia was almost as wet as Angie!

Ted and Marcia spent an hour helping Angela with her workout, but when they got ready to leave, Marcia called to Angie. "Next time I think we'll assign Ann Schmidt this job," she laughed. "You can splash her, and maybe she *will* fall in."

"I bet she'll remember to wear cheerleader uniform shorts," Angela laughed. "I guess you noticed, it's hard to be very ladylike in a skirt around the pool."

"Angie, you are leading the way for girls in athletics," said Marcia. "Some of us are beginning to realize how much you are doing for all of us."

Ted cleared his throat. "We still have a date tonight if my calendar is right," he said. "And there's a special football practice tomorrow morning," he reminded her as he left.

That night, Angie and Ted saw a movie about the world war, which gave Angela a better appreciation of what life must have been like for her father as a wartime soldier.

Later, as Angie kissed Ted good-night, she gave him an extra little squeeze. "Thanks, Ted," she said. "Thanks for getting the cheerleaders involved in supporting the swimming team. It means a lot to me."

"It means a lot to me, too," he replied. "You've earned it."

On Saturday morning, Angela's tutors were both out of town on family visits. Dressed warmly in slacks, sweater, overcoat, and bandana, Angie ran out to the Ford coupe as Ted pulled up. To keep warm on the sidelines at Strobel Field, Angie did some routines with the cheerleading squad. When she casually performed

A LADY, A CHAMPION

a standing backflip, pike position, without any assist, the cheerleaders stood in awe. Even Ann Schmidt could only mumble, "Gee whiz!"

On Saturday night Angela had dinner with Miss Amanda Foster, who listened carefully to Angie's detailed report of her activities.

"When will you meet with real Olympic coaches and some of the athletes, Angela?" asked Miss Foster, watching her protégée intently.

"In February there's a meeting in Cleveland," said Angela. "Miss Aileen Riggin will be there, as well as some of the track stars—Jesse Owens, for one."

"How will you deal with the Germans, dear?" asked Miss Foster. "They write indescribably beautiful music and poetry, but they also started a terrible war that damaged your father's life, I fear, and put a few rocks in your own young path. I'm told that Chancellor Hitler does not welcome our Negroes nor our Jews, even though some of them may be mainstays on our Olympic team."

"Me, deal with the Germans, Miss Foster?" queried Angela. "I'm just a young girl. I don't mean to be rude, ma'am, but I don't see how the Germans have anything to do with me. I'm just going to get in my lane and swim."

"We shall see, Angela. You look exactly like the model girls on the Nazi youth movement recruiting posters. But I'm sure your coaches will tell you what to do," said Miss Foster. "And they tell me you have a remarkable talent to win people's voluntary cooperation. A wonderful trait, my dear."

On Sunday, Angela and Mary went to church, but Pastor Slayton's sermon on thankfulness was very ordi-

Swimming with the Varsity

nary, using no illustrations from sports. Angela wondered if he knew that her life was still full of struggles and conflict. *Oh well,* she reasoned, *he has three hundred other people's souls to worry about besides mine.*

In December, Coach Miller scheduled varsity swimmers' workouts from 4:00-5:30 P.M. daily. At the first team meeting Captain Bill Wilkie explained the new practice of wearing bathing suits at all practices since Angela had joined the team. The male swimmers assured Angie of their respect and cooperation.

"Thank you," Angela said to all of them. "I'll try to fit in and be part of the team, but I want you to know how important each of you is to me. I need your competition, and if I make the Olympics, a part of each of you on this team will go with me to Berlin."

Bill Wilkie quickly pointed out that Angie's presence was responsible for the cheerleaders' decision to start supporting the swimmers for the first time. "This could focus a lot of community attention on swimming meets now," he said.

Angie's workout schedule was intense during the Christmas holidays, and Ted began a stiff pre-season practice schedule with the varsity basketball team.

Christmas of 1935 was the first happy one Angela had ever known. In the true spirit of Christmas, in spite of their busy schedules, both she and Ted visited every patient in the city's two hospitals who had no family to be with them for Christmas. The two of them delivered altar flowers from the churches to more than a dozen shut-ins. The shut-ins glowed in the warmth brought by the two sincere youngsters' visit.

In January, when school resumed, Angela posted a card inside her locker door, listing her five courses, her own private swimming workout time from 3:00-4:00 P.M., followed by selective workouts and time trials with the varsity swimmers.

Angela's studies were going extremely well. Her first semester grade card clearly demonstrated the results of teaming up an analytical mind with regular food and sleep, and some support and appreciation from people who cared for her.

Ted seemed to enjoy his special bonds with Angie: athletic workouts, tight schedules, high personal standards, and a sense of mission and purpose in life.

On February 18, 1936, Angela turned sixteen and celebrated by swimming the Sandusky-Fremont swimming meet. Sandusky and Fremont each had a star backstroker, and the lane markers were moved to accommodate the two usual swimmers from each school, plus Angela in the center lane. She and the two lead swimmers would swim an extra ten yards to show the crowd what the 100 meters looked like.

They would also be timed for the 100-yard distance. Officials announced that the long-standing Northern Ohio Scholastic Conference record for the 100 yards was 1:09.4.

The crowd buzzed with anticipation and it was hard to obtain silence for the start. The boys gave it their best, but Angela's high flutter kick and smooth, splashless machine-like strokes made the margin of difference. She hit the wall at the end of the fifth lap at a blistering 1:07.5, flipped around in a perfect turn, and registered a superb 1:19.6 for the 100 meters. Her time

Swimming with the Varsity

was less than half a second slower than Barbara Eastman's when she won the 1932 Olympics! Sandusky's lead backstroker clocked an impressive 1:08.1 for the 100 yards, just touching out Fremont's star, who also finished well under the conference record.

When the head official explained all the statistics, the crowd erupted into wild applause. Just then someone nudged Angela and nodded toward the spectator deck. There, at the end of the first row sat Angela's father in his wheelchair. She ran to him and hugged him while the crowd cheered, and several people cried openly. Then Angie quickly put on her robe and sat down beside her father to avoid upstaging the two boys' teams any further.

Afterward, Ted and his parents gave her a huge birthday party, making sure that her father's birthday observance with her came first. For Peter Weber, Angela's birthday brought mixed emotions: the painful memory of losing his beloved wife in childbirth mingled with his intense pride of being the father of the best-known girl in the city. At least Angela had won him a source of support and care for now.

To add to the celebration, Angela received a letter full of praise and encouragement from the Olympic star Miss Eltheda Bleibtrey in New York. Miss Bleibtrey seemed to know a lot about Angela's struggles. Angela suspected that Miss Foster had been writing some letters herself.

The following Friday, Angela was excused from school to drive with Sue Miller to Cleveland, where the U.S. Olympic Committee was conducting a preparatory session. Since Coach Miller was busy with swim team practice, his colleague from Rocky River High School in Cleveland attended the meeting with Sue and Angela.

For Angie, the high point of the meeting was seeing the still petite and trim Miss Aileen Riggin, veteran of the 1920 and 1924 Olympics. She was one of only two women to win medals in both swimming and diving. Miss Riggin was in Cleveland to organize the Billy Rose Aquacade, a lovely spectacle of synchronized swimming, diving, water fountains, water ballet, colored lights, and music. She volunteered to meet with aspiring Olympic athletes, especially to motivate female swimmers.

As the meeting progressed, Angela learned that she would leave Sandusky in June for an Olympic training camp, where she would live for a month. Then she would sail for Germany in mid July, with a stopover in France, to be in Berlin from late July through August 16. There were hundreds of details to remember. The organizers also stressed the importance of doing well in the AAU meets. The AAU women's swimming meet was in mid April at the Chicago Athletic Club.

After the meeting, there was a social time for all the athletes. Angie's heart pounded as she was introduced to the sports hero of every northern Ohioan, the track and field sensation, Jesse Owens.

"I have the clipping of your May 25th meet last summer in my scrapbook, Jesse," said Angela. "Would you autograph it if I mailed it to you?"

"Sure, Angie," said Owens, "as long as you send me your own clippings with your autograph."

Angie couldn't believe it. The man who had broken or tied six world records in less than an hour at Ann Arbor's National AAU Track Meet, knew about the big

Swimming with the Varsity

day of a Sandusky high school girl six weeks later!

"You know about me?" stammered Angie. "I mean, I'm just a school girl from Sandusky. Last summer, before Miss Foster decided to sponsor me, I—"

"You were struggling like a real champ," said Jesse, in his calm reassuring way. "I know what it's like to be on the bottom of the pile, Angela. Keep doing your best, and you'll find your dream, because someone will always come along to help you."

"Jesse—" Angie's face clouded with concern. "Will Hitler be mean, uh, bad to you?" asked Angela.

"If he is, he's just hurting himself," said the great champion. "God knows what's going on in Jesse's heart, and that's all I have to concern myself with."

"I wish you all your dreams, Jesse," whispered Angie, her eyes misting over. "I know God will watch over them for you."

The following Sunday afternoon, Angela realized again that her crown kept having unexpected thorns. The afternoon was cold and blustery when she went to Ted's house. After she was inside, she discovered that Mr. and Mrs. Gunter were out of town.

"Ted," she said, "I should go. Right now. This isn't right."

"Why?" Ted asked. "We work like dogs all week. You're just back from the Olympic prep meeting, and I'm just home from the invitationals in Toledo. I never touch you, Angie, except to kiss you good night. Besides, before long you'll be leaving for the whole summer."

"I know," said Angie, "and next fall, you go away to college. What then? We have years of waiting for each other."

A LADY, A CHAMPION

"Angie, sit down with me here, please. We have to talk," pleaded Ted.

Warning buzzers went off in Angela's head, but she cared so much for Ted, she didn't want to lose him. Cautiously, she sat on the couch beside Ted, turning expectantly toward him, not sure what to do.

Ted admired her firm figure under her soft knit sweater, the plaid wool skirt draped prettily over her legs, and her curly blonde hair pulled behind her ears with a hairband.

"Angie, kiss me," he whispered. As he pulled her toward him with his right arm, his left hand fell gently on her knee.

Angela felt strongly attracted, eager for the next move as their lips pressed warmly together. Why shouldn't she be like the other girls? Why did she always have to work hard, to deny herself, to be noble Angela who wasn't part of the crowd?

Ted's right hand gently caressed her soft hair. His breathing came fast, not at all like the disciplined athlete.

"We need each other now, or we'll never have anything," he said in a low voice.

"Please, Ted, no. Not this way," whispered Angie. "If we marry, you won't have to ask. But we have so long to go."

"Angie, we're special. We're not like those other kids," said Ted, touching her intimately but softly. "We know what our standards are. We—deserve each other. Now."

"Do you know, Ted, the result of this for a young unmarried girl?" pleaded Angela. "I'm not struggling, have you noticed? I'm praying you and I together can

Swimming with the Varsity

agree that what we're doing is wonderful, but it's not for us yet."

"It's that Miller woman, and that Pastor Bob—," said Ted, bitterly. "They really have you believing you're a saint or something."

"Ted, I care for you," said Angela. "If I've teased you into this, I apologize with all my heart. We shared a dream about the future."

"We do, Angie. We do, see?" replied Ted, drawing himself closer.

"No, Ted, we don't," said Angie, suddenly realizing that he saw his gentlemanly self-restraint with her as an argument for taking more liberties. "If you truly care for me, don't make me plead and struggle."

Sadly, reluctantly, Ted pushed himself away from her. His voice was hoarse, choked with feeling. "It's not fair. I've stood up for you, respected you," he said.

"I know. But Ted, you knew your parents wouldn't be here, so you must have meant for things to happen like this," she said, her mind whirling. "Take me home, Ted. I'm not angry, but I'm hurt. I know you are hurt, too."

"Could I see you tomorrow evening?" he asked.

"Call me, Ted. Give me time to think. You've been out with lots of girls. When you met me, I'd never been anywhere, nor done anything. Let me grow up a little. Let me seek my crown," she said.

They drove to her house in silence. She went into her room and cried, not for what Ted had done to her, but because another of her dreams had crumbled.

A few minutes later, Angie gave Sue Miller's number to the operator, and Sue answered quickly.

"Sue, I know you've spent a lot of time with me lately,

and you need your time with Coach, and I know—oh, Sue—" She began to cry.

"Angie," Sue replied, "pack an overnight bag. You can spend the night with me. I can tell things have gone wrong for you. Ted, I would guess. David is out of town tonight anyway. Pack a bag and I'll be there in ten minutes to pick you up."

Bless Sue! Angela thought. She told her father that Sue wanted her over to spend the night to keep her company.

"It's the Gunter boy, isn't it, honey?" her father asked. "Them people in the big houses, they think you owe them something if you're poor. Well, we have our pride."

"Thanks, Father. I'll be OK. And Father, I love you," Angie said, kissing him impulsively.

Girl talk kept Angela and Sue up very late that night as Angela sorted through her feelings, convictions, and goals.

Things were never the same between Angela and Ted. They had a few more dates, and respected each other too much to unload recriminations to their friends. But the beauty of their relationship had faded.

Sue Miller only gave her husband a vague explanation that Angela and Ted were facing the reality of separate demands and schedules for their futures.

Angela, at age sixteen, had been hurt by one boyfriend who never really entered her life, and now a second, who had made her think that he really shared the climb to Mount Olympus. But Ted Gunter wanted to know a side of Angela that she was keeping on reserve, probably for him, but a side to be opened *after* she had won her incorruptible crown, and not before.

Swimming with the Varsity

For the next two months, Angela worked herself mercilessly in her swimming, and each weekend she worked out at a nearby city where there was a three-meter springboard. While Angie drew closer to Mary Zimmerman and to her father, her teachers detected an intensity in her assignments that bordered on anger. But all of Angela's energy now was directed toward the AAU meet in Chicago.

On a Tuesday in mid-April, David and Sue Miller boarded the New York Central Limited with Angela at dinnertime, and they woke up next morning at the huge station in Chicago. Here everything was the big time. Nationally-famous Olympic and AAU swimmers poured in from all over: Ohio State, Yale, the Los Angeles and Chicago Swim Clubs, and many more places.

Not long into the competition, handsome Adolph Keifer stepped up before the home crowd in Chicago to start a men's qualifying heat in the 100-yard backstroke. Fifty-nine and six-tenths seconds later, he had broken the great barrier, the one-minute mark. The adoring Chicago crowd filled the giant natatorium with thunderous applause that rolled on and on. Everyone felt that Keifer, a gentleman beloved by all, would win the 100-meter backstroke race in Berlin.

After Keifer's qualifying heat, Angela met Alice Bridges from Massachusetts. She was a college student who seemed very mature, very composed. The two girls soon discovered that they both were in awe of Barbara Eastman, the reigning women's backstroke queen.

"If you make the Olympic squad, Angela," Alice told her, "you'll also have to face Hendrika Mastenbrook from Holland. She's just sixteen, like you. She's already broken several of the best times from the 1932 Olympics in freestyle and backstroke."

Angela tried to watch the more experienced women competitors to pick up tips, but she won her qualifying heat in the 100-yard backstroke with a disappointing 1:20.7. The longer pool made a big difference.

As Angela worked out in the springboard diving, she made friends with a Floridian named Katherine Rawls. Kathy Rawls was eighteen and, like Angela, hoping for a swimming medal, only in the freestyle. Her two sisters were also swimming champions and were in the meet.

Kathy introduced Angie to Dorothy Poynton, now competing under her married name, Hill. Dorothy Poynton-Hill was queen of the springboard. But the beautiful and sophisticated gold medal winner from the 1932 Los Angeles Games was very gracious to Kathy and Angela.

In the springboard diving Angela felt strong and easily made the finals. On the third night of the meet, in the three-meter board competition, Dorothy Poynton-Hill, Angela Weber, and Kathy Rawls, finished in that order, putting on a show of feminine grace and athletic skill that sent the sports writers racing to the telephone.

The next day, as Angie got set on her backstroke starting block she remembered Adolph Keifer's wise advice to her earlier. "Hold your form, Angie," he had said. "Your strength is in your style, like mine." Spurred on by his encouragement and the deafening cheers from the crowd, Angie came within three inches of upsetting the favored Barbara Eastman.

"First place, Eastman; second place, Weber; third place, Bridges," came the announcement. "Winning

Swimming with the Varsity

time is a new world record. All three top times are a new AAU record." The crowd went wild again. The three beautiful swimmers had captured the hearts of the spectators.

On the last night, at a reception for the athletes, all the medal winners exchanged addresses. They looked forward to being together in June for Olympic training camp.

The following morning, after many tearful goodbyes, Angela boarded the New York Central Limited with Coach Miller and Sue, her two AAU silver medals in her purse, and soul afire. When the train arrived at the Sandusky railroad station, dusk was falling, and a cold April wind blew off the lake.

About two hundred people gathered at the station to welcome Angela. Led by the high school cheerleading squad, the crowd chanted her name. "An-gie! An—gie! An—gie!" they shouted. "A, A, A-A-A; N, N, N-N-N; G, G, G-G-G; I, I, I-I-I; E, E, E-E-E!" The cheerleaders adapted a Sandusky football cheer.

As Angela stepped off the train, Mary Zimmerman and Pastor Bob Slayton each gave her a hug. Then Angie rode in a horn-blowing parade to the little house where her father waited on the front porch.

Fame had reached out now and changed Angela forever. But tomorrow morning she would be a tenth-grader again, with only two months more of school and one month of Olympic camp to prepare her for the world's greatest effort to expand human abilities, to seek the way of the gods.

Angela would have to work hard if she wanted to change her two AAU silver medals into Olympic gold.

SIX
Being for Girls Everywhere

Not long after Angela returned from the meet, Miss Foster invited her to dinner at a lovely restaurant over on the Marblehead Peninsula. A uniformed chauffeur drove Angela and her benefactor to the restaurant in Miss Foster's limousine.

"Angela, how much will you have to improve to win a gold medal?" asked Miss Foster as they rode along. "Are there European girls who can give you a race?"

"Yes, Miss Foster," Angela answered. "The Dutch girls are great. And times don't stand still, you know. The other American girls will improve by next August," she said.

"What will you do to improve your speed and your dives?" persisted Miss Foster.

"For the swimming, there's no substitute for laps, laps, laps, and then sprints, sprints, sprints," Angela laughed. "There's always room for technique, and other little details. But my body is still developing. Each week I have a tiny bit more power since you've got me eating right."

"And the diving, Angela? Does improvement in your swimming power help or hurt your diving?" asked Miss Foster.

"More body power helps, but as I put on weight, I have to keep changing the timing on my dives. My upper torso, as Coach Miller calls it, is heavier, so it makes me rotate faster. I guess polish and timing are the most important." Angela fidgeted in her seat, wondering if she was boring Miss Foster with too many details.

"I don't mean to cross-examine you, Angela dear," said Miss Foster. "It's just that your success has made a part of me come alive after a very long wait!"

Miss Foster and her protégeé shared a lovely dinner at a fancy restaurant on Lake Erie. As they ate, they watched a beautiful sunset color the little waves lapping on the rocks outside the dining room window. Angela felt relaxed and happy with Miss Foster. She knew that her victories were as important to her kindly sponsor as they were to herself.

On the drive home, the conversation shifted. "You must trust me that your father will be all right during your long absence this summer," said Miss Foster. "Even though I've taken some of the work off your shoulders, I know you do a lot to keep his life organized, and he utterly dotes on you. But to do well in Berlin, you must be free of worry. I have several extra people lined up to fill his life. Also, upon your return, I will discuss plans with you for finishing your education. You must not live in fear of being thrown back into your old situation. My attorney has already taken steps to see that it cannot happen."

Being for Girls Everywhere

They drove awhile in silence, and then Angela brought up a subject that was painful to her.

"You have done so much for me, to give my dreams a chance, and . . . I wondered if I should tell you about my boyfriend," said Angie.

"A girl is entitled to privacy on that subject, Angela," said Miss Foster. "Especially a girl who sets her standards on mountaintops as high as you do! I pity the boys."

"Well, Miss Foster, you know Ted Gunter and his family," said Angela. "We were pretty serious. I thought we shared the same dreams and goals, but we don't. I guess we're just friends, now."

"And you must keep the rest to yourself, Angela," said Miss Foster. "You are so honest and dedicated. You once called me your champion, but it's the reverse, dear. You are like a knight to me," she said. "Amanda Foster, in her tottering old age, has found herself a girl knight to joust for her on the field of honor." She chuckled. Angela smiled to know that somehow she had pleased Miss Foster in some unexpected way.

The next day, Sunday, Angela spent the afternoon with Pastor Bob Slayton and his wife. There had obviously been talk among many of her supporters about who was going to take care of Angela's father during her two-month absence, because Pastor Bob also tried to reassure Angela that her father would be looked in on frequently. "Angie," he said, "we just want you to clear your mind for the business of swimming and diving."

The next day, Coach Miller told Angela he wanted her to have a week of reduced workouts and two weeks with no time trials. He arranged for Angela to be excused from school once in the morning and once in the afternoon, to swim with junior high girls. Then a select few would be allowed to work out with her from 3:00 to 4:00, following which Angela could go home early for the first time in seven months.

The next day, Angie checked in at Miss Hartung's English class and received a pass. Then she rode her bicycle to the junior high school and within a few minutes was swimming before the awed gaze of thirty-two seventh grade girls. After demonstrating the three basic competition strokes, she mounted the one-meter diving board and gave examples of the three sets of dives.

"Angela," said the swimming teacher, "the class would like to ask you some questions. Why don't you stand on the end of the diving board so they can all hear you."

Many hands shot up. Angela had awakened a dormant competitive drive in girls throughout the district around Sandusky.

"When did you first know that you were fast? How could you tell?" asked one girl.

"In scratch races, mostly against boys, down at Battery Park," Angela replied. "Starting when I was ten—that summer I'd go to Battery Park and swim. It made the boys mad when I beat them," she said.

The girls laughed.

"Where did you learn to dive?" several asked in chorus.

"I watched the boys from the high school diving team at Battery Park a few times," answered Angela. "And right here in this pool, three years ago, I practiced on this board and asked the teachers to help me."

Being for Girls Everywhere

"Did Miss Joiner teach you how to dive when you were our age?" was the next question.

Angela smiled at the teacher who had been a real friend to her. "Miss Alice Joiner taught me a lot," Angela answered. "She encouraged me to get coaching, and I think she had a lot to do with getting Coach David Miller to consider coaching a girl swimmer and diver," answered Angela.

Miss Joiner smiled to herself. Long ago she had vowed never to tell Angie that at first Coach Miller had utterly rejected the idea of coaching a pretty little poor girl. Miss Joiner took the risk of setting up an accidental meeting between Angela and Sue Miller. When Coach Miller's wife began taking a young girl to Battery Park for swimming, and asking him for tips on how to make her swim faster, David's coaching instinct took over. That's when Angela started the secret workouts in the junior high school pool at night and on weekends.

"Is it true you can beat the boys on the swimming team in all the events?" asked a girl.

"I'm not really sure," said Angela, not wanting to boast. "I haven't gone head-to-head against all of them, but remember, someone in the next lane is always getting faster. It's better to let your swimming do the talking."

There was a moment of reflective silence.

"Aren't you scared when you spin around so close to the end of the board on your dives?" someone asked.

"I'll tell you a girl's secret about that," said Angela. "One time, one of the football players was telling some guys that I wasn't really an athlete like they are, because he said that in football there's danger in getting hit by other players, whereas in swimming and diving

103

you just perform by yourself. Well, one of the guys asked him to do the one-and-one-half gainer from the three-meter board. That's the one where you go off frontwards, then somersault backwards toward the board. It's plenty dangerous, because you can't see the board while you're setting up the somersault. Well, anyway, that answer shut the guy up."

"My mother says you used to stay home and take care of your father, but you don't any more," said an outspoken young girl. "And she says your bathing suit—," she giggled, "—shows way too much of you."

A ripple of talk and giggles among the girls, indicated that this topic had been discussed between many mothers and daughters. Angela suppressed her anger and tried to choose her words carefully.

"Olympic athletes have to live while they train, but they're not supposed to earn a salary or they're considered professionals. So, they get a sponsor, or their families support them. Miss Amanda Foster is sponsoring me because my family is very poor. About my bathing suit—it is just like the ones used in the Miss America Contest and in girls' swim meets all over the world. I, like most athletes, am a person with high standards."

"Bravo, Angela!" said Miss Joiner, amazed at her poise. "Girls, Angela has given you some great answers to tough questions. And these are the kinds of questions that are sometimes thrown at girls who dare to be athletes. Right now you can't appreciate it all, but try to remember what she has said. Now, here are the names of the girls who may swim with Angela at 3:00 this afternoon."

While Miss Joiner finished, Angela quickly dressed and rode back over to the high school. But in the after-

Being for Girls Everywhere

noon, she returned for a repeat performance with the eighth grade girls.

Angela stayed around after the question and answer session, swimming laps and giving tips and encouragement to six swimmers and divers who showed potential.

The next day in geometry, Mr. Thomas told Angela he would be giving her a series of advanced exercises in geometry and algebra that she could work on at home at her own speed. "Our Saturday tutoring sessions are over now," he said.

"Have I done something wrong, Mr. Thomas?" asked Angela.

"Quite the opposite!" Her teacher laughed. "You are one of the best geometry students we have now, and others need my time. Mrs. Thomas and I have one request, however," he said, looking shyly at his desk.

"Yes, sir?" Angela asked.

"We'd like a photograph taken with you, and we want you to autograph it for us," said the man who never spoke to her of anything except lines, angles, and lesson assignments.

"I'll be glad to," said Angela. "If I do well in the Olympics, Mr. Thomas, please remember that you are the one who taught me that a straight line really is the shortest distance between two points."

When Angela arrived at her English class, she found that things were winding down there, too. Miss Lois Hartung assigned Angela to write little biographies of several famous Olympic stars.

"The truth is, that you are the only one around here who knows anything about the inner workings of the

Olympics," said Miss Hartung. "And our tutoring sessions, for the rest of the year, will be to work on your Olympic biographies. You're making an A in your course without any special help."

As spring flowers popped up in Sandusky gardens, the newspaper discovered that Angela was interesting hometown story material. Although she was photographed in her bathing suit in dozens of poses, Sue Miller kept a close eye on the proceedings and went down to the newspaper office regularly to see which pictures were actually going to be used. The photos, with accompanying stories, featuring Angela as a struggling poor girl who made good in the American tradition, brought out new support and some unexpected opposition.

At an overcrowded meeting of the chamber of commerce, someone proposed having an "Angela Weber Day" to publicize the opening of Cedar Point Amusement Park across Sandusky Bay. The beach there was world famous, and the businessmen hoped such a celebration would stimulate sales in swimwear and beach supplies.

Mrs. Dorothy Ogletree, having heard rumors that the "Angela Weber Day" idea would be proposed, wrote an angry letter to the chamber of commerce. "I have something to say on behalf of decency in Sandusky," she wrote.

Coach Miller reluctantly took Angela to the meeting to help defend her position.

As the meeting progressed, Mrs. Ogletree stared across the room at Angela, making the young girl very uncomfortable.

The business development subcommittee reported

Being for Girls Everywhere

the need to stimulate retail sales during the summer season, and presented a plan for Angela to appear in a series of newspaper ads and radio commercials. After discussions of possible fees, production costs, and community perceptions, the floor was opened to public discussion.

Mrs. Ogletree immediately marched to the podium. "On behalf of the women of Sandusky," she said haughtily, "I wish to make a statement about decency. For two years I have watched this town make a fool of itself over a poor girl who can swim fast—not that being poor is anything personal against Angela, mind you—"

"Really, Mrs. Ogletree," the chairman objected. "Our meeting is not a place for you to criticize other citizens."

"You asked for public participation, and now you are going to listen," Mrs. Ogletree insisted. "Mothers all over this town have seen a young girl in a skimpy bathing suit, leaping, swimming, and grinning, but always exposing herself shamefully, until our daughters are rebelling against modest standards. And now, our schools have this mermaid creature teaching insubordination to junior high girls!"

"Really, Mrs. Ogletree," interrupted the chairman. "This is a matter for the board of education."

"It's a matter for decent people," retorted Mrs. Ogletree. "You gentlemen are discussing the idea of placing a pretty sixteen-year-old girl in a revealing photograph to arouse business interest. What kind of interest do you really think you will be arousing? And at whose expense?"

David Miller found himself wishing that Sue had been

able to attend. He knew that he was no match for Mrs. Ogletree's slander technique. Angela needed a woman to defend her.

As Mrs. Ogletree resumed her seat, the room grew uncomfortably silent.

Slowly, Angela raised her hand. "Would it be all right for that sixteen-year-old girl to speak?" she asked.

"Of course, Angela. Come on up," said the chairman. "Since you're the subject of all this discussion, we can hardly refuse your opinion."

Suddenly, the crowd in the packed little auditorium stood and cheered as if Angela had just won a race.

Mrs. Ogletree bristled at the public display of affection for Angela.

"Mr. Chairman," said Angela, trying to remember protocol, "thank you for letting me speak. I am honored that you let me come, and honored that you think I could somehow help business in Sandusky. We all know the times are hard, and many people aren't sure where their next meal is coming from."

The room hushed. Everyone listened with rapt attention. The adults who did not know Angela were amazed at her clear, restrained, but confident way of speaking.

"I respect what Mrs. Ogletree is saying," she continued.

Mrs. Ogletree snorted dramatically.

"That is why I have always tried to set an example of decency and honesty," she continued. "The truth is that I'm not an Olympic star yet. An American Amateur Athletics Union silver medalist is not considered by most people to be a true athletic champion, although all of you here in Sandusky have been so kind to me. The Olympic Committee warned all of us against doing any-

Being for Girls Everywhere

thing before the Games that could be taken as earning money through sports. They also warned us not to raise a public ruckus about our appearance in our bathing suits."

"Angela," said the chairman with relief, "you are an example to us all in clear thinking and modesty. When you return from Berlin, your chamber of commerce will be happy to receive guidance on how a famous Olympic star can help build up business around her hometown without violating Olympic rules. Angela Weber, on behalf of the business community, I want you to know that we are all very proud of you. Do I have a motion to put this plan on the shelf for now?"

The chairman's awkward little speech prompted wild applause, and the trouble was temporarily averted.

Two days later, Angela was called out of biology class to the principal's office. When Angela arrived, Miss Foster sat opposite the principal, clutching her silver-handled cane in her strong, withered hands.

"Come in, Angela," said the principal, "and ask Coach Miller to step in, too," he called to the secretary in the outer office. Angela wondered what was coming next. All her time lately seemed to be taken up by people worried about her, yet none of it had anything to do with swimming or diving.

The principal gave a deep sigh and then began. "There is a school board meeting tonight to discuss plans for graduation, Angela," he said.

"But sir, I'm only a tenth-grader," Angie said quickly.

"Unfortunately, Angela," said Miss Foster, "you are now famous. And when you are famous, people make you part of the public's business. One school board member thinks you should be honored at the graduation. Another opposed it because you're not a graduating senior. And Mrs. Ogletree is on the agenda to speak about her favorite topic—bathing suits."

"What if I just stay home from graduation?" asked Angela. "A lot of tenth-graders don't go. I could always say I'm packing for Olympic training camp since I leave the very next day."

"That's a generous thought, Angela," said the principal. "You have no idea how much we appreciate the fact that our most famous student is also modest."

"Well, we're going to do more than just flatter her, this time," said Miss Foster. "If I were Angela, after all this foolishness, I'm not sure I'd want to take part in anything more at all in Sandusky."

Coach Miller put his hand on Angie's shoulder. "Angela, suppose you come to the board meeting with Sue and me tonight, but let others speak for you this time," he said. "Actually, I think it would be a very sporting gesture for you to attend the graduation and sit well back in the audience. I agree with you that graduation is not the place for you to be recognized."

That night, the Sandusky Board of Education, accustomed to having three or four people attend its meetings, had to adjourn for fifteen minutes and move to the City Hall Auditorium to accommodate the crowd.

One board member proposed that the school board honor Angela with a special medal of achievement on the eve of her departure for Olympic training camp. Acknowledging that, upon her return, the city government and news media would lay first claim on honoring Angela if she performed well, he wanted the people who had educated Angela to recognize her first.

Being for Girls Everywhere

Coach Miller took the podium next and he read a short prepared statement in which Angela thanked the board for their support and interest in her career, but asked that she be allowed to attend the graduation with Mrs. Miller, sit in the audience, and join with all of Sandusky in honoring the graduating class of 1936.

The school board voted to accept this plan by asking the originator of the motion to withdraw it.

When Mrs. Dorothy Ogletree asked to speak, a chorus of catcalls indicated her lack of popularity. Yet some in the audience seemed to enjoy watching her take on the board of education.

"Night after night, weekend after weekend," said Mrs. Ogletree, "this board of education, which is sworn to educate our youth, has allowed a coach in its employ to take a young girl out of her classes, out of her home, indeed, out of town, to seek fame as an athlete. Not surprisingly, with financial help from one of the area's wealthiest persons, the girl has achieved a degree of notoriety. But at what price? And how shall this board justify that the girl is now seen as a heroine among junior and senior high school girls? Also can anyone deny that commercial exploitation of her God-given prettiness, dressed in a manner more suited to Hollywood hussies, has already begun among our business leaders?

"When will this board of education take a stand? A stand that its male teachers may not sneak around at night with vulnerable young girls from—excuse me, but yes—from the lower class? When will the board discharge its obligation to teach young motherless girls, who have an ailing father, to stay home and care for the family, as God intended women to do?

"I do not care to hear your graduation plans," sniffed Mrs. Ogletree. "I want to hear what you're doing about disciplinary measures."

Mrs. Ogletree sat down, and utter silence reigned.

Angela leaned toward Sue and whispered. "How would you like me to forget the ladylike ways you've been teaching me, and to run up there and knock her teeth down her throat?"

"It's what she deserves, baby, but let someone else do it for you," whispered Sue, squeezing Angela's arm. "Come to think of it, it would be fun to watch you do that."

Sue snickered as they both turned to see the door of the meeting room swing open. Angela gasped as a uniformed nurse and Amanda Foster's chauffeur pushed Angie's father into the room in his wheelchair. Behind them came Miss Foster herself, erect and proud.

"I wish to speak, Mr. Chairman," announced Miss Foster.

Sue whispered to Angie. "President Roosevelt himself wouldn't dare deny Miss Foster her moment at city hall," she said.

The crowd hushed in anticipation of the fireworks about to erupt as the city's wealthiest citizen did public battle with a self-appointed defender of the public morals.

Miss Foster took her place behind the lectern. "Sixty years ago this summer," she said, her voice loud and clear, "I arrived in the same city where Angela Weber will represent herself, her school, her family, her city, and her country in the world's greatest athletic contest. Berlin was the educational mountaintop of that day,

Being for Girls Everywhere

but I quickly learned that a girl could not be allowed to swim. Although my father was worth millions and could well afford to send me to school anywhere in the world, thanks to the petty little minds such as you have heard tonight, I was prevented from swimming.

"If people who think like Mrs. Ogletree ran this country, not a woman in this room would be able to swim at Cedar Point this summer. Nor wear shorts. Nor wear the comfortable dresses you have on right now. Nor smoke a cigarette, although I can't see what good that might be.

"Some of you know Angela Weber. Most of you think you do, but you don't know the real Angela Weber. For five years Angela fed, kept house, cared for—in short, did everything for her father. He is here tonight, so that no more false witness may be borne in public. Not one of you in this room, certainly not I, has ever had to live like that, nor discharged so impossible a task with such fidelity. God endowed Angela with beauty, brains, and two glorious talents, which Mrs. Ogletree is seeking to deny her.

"Yes, ladies and gentlemen," Miss Foster continued, "in my old age, I took on Angela's training and the care of her father—not for me, but to use my wealth to carry out God's purpose. Mr. Weber is here, and he can tell you that his daughter still stays with him, still cares for him, still adores him, but as a daughter, not as an indentured servant.

"And now, Angela's persistence has paid off. She is part of our national treasury of great athletes. Soon she will carry your flag of honor to athletic greatness in Berlin. The world will be watching to see if the democratic nations produce great champions or spoiled people, as

Mr. Hitler purports. Angela will be there, making your statement."

Miss Foster cleared her throat dramatically. "I believe," she said firmly, "that we have had enough of Mrs. Ogletree's slander, her innuendo, and unsubstantiated charges. If she is prepared to take this matter to court, so be it. Otherwise, I say, let's free Angela to do what we are sending her to do.

"I hope you will join Angela, and the Millers, and me in paying tribute to the graduating class of 1936. And in August, I trust this town will remember the sacrifices of a girl who dares to struggle, yes to struggle, for an incorruptible crown."

There was a long pause as Miss Foster marched out of the auditorium, her little procession following her.

The chairman of the school board stood and fumbled for words. "I think all our business has been accomplished," he said feebly. "Will a member please the chair by offering a resolution of appreciation to Miss Angela Weber for the leadership she has provided our school district, and also, the customary resolution of commendation to the graduating class of 1936?"

Mrs. Dorothy Ogletree stalked angrily out the side door, her face aflame.

One of the members obliged, and both resolutions passed 5-0 without discussion.

The chairman sighed with relief. "Thank you all for coming. Meeting adjourned," he said.

Angela followed Sue Miller through the door in a daze. In the hallway outside, person after person stopped to talk and shake Angela's hand.

"You're OK, Angie."

"We all love you."

Being for Girls Everywhere

"We're all in your corner, Angie," each said in his own way.

The last of the well-wishers was Mrs. Schmidt, who paused awkwardly in front of Angela with her daughter, Ann.

"Angela, this is difficult for me, but I want Mrs. Miller to hear what I must say to you. I have wronged you," said Mrs. Schmidt, "wronged you terribly, and have turned my daughter against you. We have both tormented you, but I've caused it. Will you accept my sincere apology? I'm not trying to excuse myself, but I knew your mother, and there was a time when I didn't get a job at a hospital because your mother got the job instead. I have taken out my malice on you, and neither of you deserved it. Oh, forgive a bitter woman, Angela."

Angie put her hands on Mrs. Schmidt's shoulders and looked into her eyes.

"God forgives wrong, Mrs. Schmidt," Angie replied, swallowing a lump in her throat. "Surely I can't carry a grudge. I never knew Mother at all, but I think she would understand and forgive. I do," she said with difficulty.

"Bless you," said Mrs. Schmidt. "I hope we can show you our friendship in the future."

"That was really something, Angie," said Sue on the way out. "I've lived in this town all my life, and I've never seen anything like it."

"More than anything I want to feel that people are with me when I go to Berlin, Sue," said Angie. "I know it's impossible for you and Coach to go along, but I want the thoughts and good wishes of everyone to go with me.

The next day, the president of the senior class came

to Angela's homeroom and thanked her for her written statement at the school board meeting, reserving honor for the seniors. "You can be sure," he said, "that the Class of 1936 is with you. You'll be getting something to prove it, but please don't let anyone know I told you. It's a surprise, and it comes from the hearts of a lot of people."

Angela thanked him, but wished that all the political aspects of her Olympic dreams would just disappear.

In history class that day, Angie found that the readings assigned by her English teacher on Olympic stars of the past, would be doubly helpful. Her spring history report was to be titled, "The History of the Modern Olympiads." She suspected that her teachers were working out the assignments to minimize her workload.

After giving her report on modern Olympic athletes to the English class, she repeated it for the history class by popular demand. Angela had learned about how the Olympics started, about women swimmers and divers, and of course about Olympians who had to overcome great obstacles in life to become athletes.

She told her classmates how the French Baron Pierre de Coubertin had admired the ancient Greeks in their quest to honor the gods. The Greeks had even cancelled wars in order to have their Games between the city-states. In 1896, she reported, a small group of daring Americans, mostly students from Harvard and Princeton, had gone to Athens for the first Modern Olympiad and had started a tradition of American supremacy in track and field.

"Women's sports," said Angela, "were rather new, and America was one of the leading nations in devel-

Being for Girls Everywhere

oping their women's swimming potential. Women's swimming had come to the Olympics at the Stockholm Games of 1912, but the American women took charge in swimming and diving at the 1920 Antwerp Games."

Angie reported that there were strong European challengers now, and she would soon be facing the greatest of them. But she also told of the role models she had discovered, athletes whose dedication would inspire her when the way seemed too hard.

She learned about the Reverend Eric Liddell, former Olympian and now a missionary in China, experiencing the terrors of war and civil disturbance. His goal was to win the incorruptible crown. Medals alone were not the goal. Medals were proof that you were the best in the world, at one thing, one time. The incorruptible crown was Angela's goal, too, she said. She wanted to be God's athlete as the Reverend Liddell had been.

There were others, too, Angela reported. Ray Ewry, from Indiana, had fought back from crippling polio to win an all-time record of ten Olympic gold medals. Glenn Cunningham would be seeking the gold medal in Berlin in the 1500-meter race. Glenn's legs had been damaged so severely in his boyhood by an exploding stove that the doctors said he'd never walk again. Jesse Owens, from Cleveland, had triumphed over poverty and prejudice, and he, like Cunningham, would soon be Angela's teammate.

When Angela finished reading her report to the second class, the students at Sandusky High School had a glimpse of the magnificent people who were Olympians, and the spiritual commitment of the pretty girl who moved among them every day, yet who somehow was removed from them by a sense of mission.

During the last week of May, Angela received a long letter about training camp from the Olympic Committee. It listed what to bring, how to act, and costs to be paid by the athletes. There were even rules about sponsoring bathing suits, track shoes, and soft drinks. Coach Miller let Angela skip her workout one afternoon so he could take her to the newspaper editor's office. The news editor called in his sports editor, and Angela gave these two gentlemen a copy of the Olympic rules she had received, so that the reporting staff could understand announcements and controversial foreign press commentary on the Games. She also furnished them with a copy of her Olympics report to enable the Sandusky paper to better interpret the results from Berlin.

The following week, Angela sat with Sue Miller in the Sandusky Junior High School Gymnasium auditorium for the graduation of the class of 1936. When Ted Gunter crossed the stage to receive his diploma, Angela joined the audience of hundreds in enthusiastically cheering Sandusky's finest team athlete of the decade. Ted was bound for Ohio State University.

Angela was bound for the Olympics. The next morning, she awoke early and packed her one trunk and two suitcases allowed by the Olympic Committee. The housekeeper planned a special farewell lunch for her and her father, knowing that the Millers would take her to the train station at 2:30.

About 10:00 A.M. the American Express truck arrived to take Angela's trunk. As the trunk went out the door Angie finally grasped the reality that she was leaving home for a long time.

At lunch her father was unusually cheerful. "You have

promised to write me every day," Angela reminded him. "I gave you a list of all the addresses with all the dates," she said.

Her father smiled. "I have your picture on my dresser and all your medals in the big oval shape on that corkboard thing you and Mary put up in the living room," he said. "There's a hole in the center of the oval, baby, and I'll look at it every day, thinking about the medals you're going to put in the center."

"Father, you'll still love me if I don't bring a medal home, won't you?" asked Angela.

"With all my heart, baby. We'll get by, you and I," he said. "The medal I got from my time against the Germans— Remember Angie, it was for savin' a couple American guys, not for killin' Germans. I don't hate 'em for what they done to me."

"That helps so much, Father," said Angela. "I've been warned that they may treat our Negro and Jewish teammates badly. It's not right, but I'll try not to make the same mistake and hate them back."

"This is our last lunch together for ages, honey, and we're talkin' like preachers or something," said Pete Weber. "I just want you to know you're the champ. You don't owe no one winnin' any medals. You just do your best. Enjoy your trip. I've worshiped the ground you walked on even if I haven't been much good to you."

Angela got up from her chair and hugged her father. "Oh, Father, life has been hard for us, and every night I ask God to watch over us both," she said. "I guess that prayer means even more now."

After lunch, they sat quietly in the living room, chatting as if nothing special were happening, each not wanting the other to have a parting recollection of tears

A LADY, A CHAMPION

and sadness. Soon there was a tap on the screen door. Angela looked out to see the Millers, Pastor Bob, and Miss Amanda Foster, all on the little front porch.

"It looks like the going-away committee is here, baby," said Father.

Angela opened the door, surprised to see anyone other than Coach Miller and Sue.

"Angela, we're invading your privacy because we love you." Miss Foster chuckled. "I brought Pastor Bob, too. The truth is that we have something special to do here."

"Angela has shared an idea with me, Mr. Weber, and I think it's wonderful," added Pastor Bob. "I know it may be painful for you, but please let Angela tell you about it."

"Sure, baby, what do you want?" asked her father.

"In the center of this corkboard, right in the center with all my swimming and diving medals around the outside—"

"Yes, baby," said Father. "I told you at lunch I love your board with all the medals."

"But in the center, Father, I want to put two more," she said. "I want to put Mother's nursing cap badge, the one from her college, right next to your Silver Star from the Great War."

Pete Weber's eyes glistened. "You want to do that, Angela? Mother and me? Mother's old badge—" His voice broke off.

Angela darted into the next room and took the two insignia from her father's upper bureau drawer. Back in the living room, she mounted the bronze medical badge and the red, white, and blue ribbon with the five-pointed star. Nothing could have symbolized her parents' lives more eloquently.

120

Being for Girls Everywhere

Pastor Bob seemed very moved. "May we join hands to ask God's blessing?" he asked.

They all formed a little semi-circle, with Angela and her father in the center.

"Our heavenly Father," said Pastor Bob, "bless Angela as she goes to Berlin seeking athletic honors in your name. Watch over her father, Lord. Keep him safe until her return. Angela has symbolically honored her parents where she displays the glory of the talent you've vested in her being. Bless her. Guard these people, dear Lord, and hear Angela's special prayer, Amen."

"Dear Lord," Angela prayed, "show me the path to my incorruptible crown. No matter how I do, help me above all else to honor my father and my mother. If I put an Olympic medal on this board, dear God, let it be a piece of the crown. May it say that I am your athlete, God's athlete, and let me wear my incorruptible crown so long as I shall live. Amen."

Angela hugged her father for a long moment, then quickly kissed Miss Foster and Pastor Bob on the cheek. Grabbing a suitcase, she stepped through the door, then turned to look back at her father. Tears streamed from her eyes, but a determined smile brightened her face.

"Good-bye, Father. God bless you!" she said. She turned quickly and walked out to the waiting Hudson and got in.

Pete Weber could barely see the Hudson pull away. His eyes were full of tears. He wheeled himself to the corkboard where the oval ring of medals surrounded the two insignias that encompassed his whole life.

"Angie said, 'Honor my father and my mother,'" he

repeated. "Honor my father and my mother."

He sat and stared at the corkboard for a long time. His mind was in a world far from Sandusky that he could neither describe nor share with any living person.

SEVEN
Olympic Training Camp

Angela pushed her nose against the cool pane of glass, watching out the window of the New York Central Pullman car bound for New York. Coach Miller and Sue seemed to shrink and then disappear as the train took the first long curve.

Angie had been aboard a Pullman once before, just two months earlier. In fact, this same train had carried her west to Chicago with the Millers, to AAU stardom, where she earned a sure place on the U.S. Olympic team. But this time she was alone. She would miss the Millers terribly. Summer would be nearly over when she returned.

Reluctantly, Angie turned away from the window and looked around the Pullman car. The double-facing seats, which would later convert into an upper and a lower bunk, had two occupants. A couple of older ladies, en route from Chicago to New York to visit relatives, chatted pleasantly. The ladies were very friendly and made an effort to include Angela in the conversa-

A LADY, A CHAMPION

tion by asking her destination. They seemed pleased that Angela would be with them all the way to New York.

The train flew through Vermillion, then jerked to a stop in the next town. "E-ler-ya," the conductor announced. All Angie could think of was that this was one of Sandusky's arch rivals in sports.

When the train reached the Cleveland Terminal, there was a long wait and much activity. After the train finally pulled out, Angela heard the conductor call, "Dinner is served in the dining car!" The two ladies, protective of their young traveling partner, invited Angela to join them at dinner. She was glad to have company. Pangs of homesickness already tore at her stomach.

When they reached the dining car, Angela admired the elegantly set tables with starched white linen, heavy china, and silverplate. As they ate together, the two ladies asked Angela more about her trip.

"Will you be staying with relatives?" one asked.

"No, just in a dormitory," Angela replied, wondering how much to say.

"A dormitory? Why you must be going to boarding school! But in mid-June, dear, that's most unusual."

"We'll be staying at a girls' college dorm that's empty for the summer," explained Angela. "I'm going to train with the Olympic team."

"Olympia, how nice," said the second lady. "You'll have to change trains at Grand Central Station then. It's quite a long way to Olympia."

"I'm on the U.S. Olympic team," said Angela, trying not to show any impatience. "The women's swimming team. We'll train in New York for a month, and then go by ocean liner to Berlin, Germany, for the Olympic Games."

Olympic Training Camp

"So you'll be going to Germany—such a long trip for a young girl alone," persisted the first lady.

"Mildred, I don't think we have fully understood what Angela is telling us," said the other. "She's not just taking a trip. She's on the American Olympic team, you know. Remember, Mildred? Back in '32? Remember when that nice Vice President Curtis was at the Games in Los Angeles?"

Angela wondered if she should say anything more. Maybe it was all a hoax. Maybe there were no Olympic Games. Here were two well-dressed ladies, obviously accustomed to travel, who scarcely seemed to have heard of the Olympics.

"It will be so nice for a lovely young girl like you to accompany the American team to Germany," said the first lady. "It's so exciting when the cheerleaders do that jumping and the somersaults. Don't your legs get cold at the football games, dear?"

"I don't think there are any cheerleaders with the Olympic teams," said Angela. "I'm a swimmer and a diver. Other athletes will be there for track and field, shooting, eques—, equestri—, horseback riding, and the other sports."

"My dear girl," said the second lady, "we've made a dreadful error. You're an athletics star, probably famous in the newspapers, and we thought you were a high school cheerleader. It's all so very new, you see."

"I do recall my husband, Ralph, reading aloud at the breakfast table . . . in April, I think it was," said the first lady. "A young girl from Sandusky—why she must be you! You nearly beat the Eastman woman, the glamorous one who was champion out at Los Angeles. And you're so young! And so pretty!"

A LADY, A CHAMPION

Once again Angela had to fit her identity into someone else's way of thinking. Why did she always have to explain what she was and what she was doing? Again, the initial reaction from older women had been the same. They could not grasp the idea that she was a real athlete, much less a star. When they did finally get it straight, there was always a wistful tone, a kind of unexpressed feeling that some time in the past the older women might have wanted to be athletes, too, but it wasn't the thing to do.

Next morning, after the sleeper compartment was raised in preparation for entering Grand Central Station, Angela bade her companions good-bye and found a redcap who helped her carry her two suitcases to a taxi. As she fished in her purse for the address, she got her first taste of New York cab driver slang. "Truthfully," she recalled later in her diary, "I never understood one word the man said."

By mid-morning, Angela was sitting on her bed in a college dorm, chatting excitedly with other young women at the training camp. It wasn't really a camp, but a college facility. She quickly met members of the track and field team, the fencing team, the gymnastics team, and of course, some swimmers and divers. Angie was especially pleased to see Kathy Rawls again.

Talk ranged from important subjects like possible political opposition in Berlin, to event schedules, to questions on the laundry service. Angela told them about the two ladies who thought she was a cheerleader headed for Germany. Then a tall, muscular young woman from the track team related how the Pullman porter reluctantly let her help him unstick a jammed upper bunk so the car would be made up as they en-

Olympic Training Camp

tered the terminal. The girls laughed and talked until it was time to go to their first meeting.

In a large conference room they experienced their first of many meetings about conduct rules and the training schedules. Immediately, a controversy arose over seeming inequities. The older single women had to observe curfew hours while the married athletes could stay with their husbands. Angela could not see why this was so important, but she kept quiet.

That night, Angela wrote postcards to Mary Zimmerman and Pastor Bob Slayton, and letters to her father, the Millers, and Miss Amanda Foster. By the time she finished writing in her diary, it was 11:00. *This isn't going to work*, Angie thought. She decided to write one letter and one card per night, a practice which within two weeks would become one letter *or* one card each night.

On the first morning of pre-Olympic training, the unequal preparation among the women swimmers and divers became apparent. Most of them lived near athletic clubs or colleges which had a metric pool. Angela quickly realized that, in spite of her early struggles, once she began training seriously, Coach Miller's excellent technique prepared her well.

Angela enjoyed the Olympic training atmosphere of total commitment. She loved being among people who thrilled in training to perfection. Top name national coaches helped Angie now, but the more they learned about how Coach David Miller had brought his protégée along with limited time and training facilities, the more they respected his training program for her.

On the third day, Head Coach Robert Kiphuth assembled the swimmers and divers for a team meeting.

"Welcome to the Olympic championship team," he began. "We have dominated this sport since the beginning, and this time we have a tough job on our hands."

The athletes waited for Coach Kiphuth's analysis of the situation, knowing that he was the finest coach in the country, perhaps in the world.

"We've lost a lot of our freestyle strength from the Los Angeles Games," he said, "and some of you older swimmers and divers know that the Japanese have been coming on fast. All of you have seen clippings about the Dutch swimmers, especially the women. The Germans and Danes will be tough, too."

Angela thought about how little most people in Sandusky knew about these sporting developments. This was another whole world.

"In this XIth Olympiad," said Coach Kiphuth, "you're going to compete in the finest natatorium ever built. It seats 20,000 spectators, and 25,000 with standing room."

Angela's eyes widened. *That's more than the entire population of Sandusky*, she thought.

Coach Kiphuth continued. "The Germans have spared no cost. And you're going to hear a lot of politics and propaganda, some of it quite nasty. I want every swimmer to set the best possible example of the athletes' oath, both on and off the field. We are pledging ourselves to honor both the sport and the athletes. How you act, what you say, even how you look—all of it's important."

"I think they want us to behave well," Kathy Rawls whispered to Angela.

"You swimmers and divers have been identified by

Olympic Training Camp

the press as a glamor team," said the coach. "That's nice, but it also means that many people will have their eyes on you, and will be making judgments about you," he warned. "Now, let's get down to business. All divers will train together, and all swimmers will train together. Two of the women, Rawls and Weber, are both swimmers and divers. Today, you two are divers. We have a special workout planned. Let's get to it!"

Angela and Kathy followed Dorothy Poynton-Hill, Velma Clancy Dunn, and the men divers to a nearby college gym where a team of gymnastics coaches waited to help them.

"We're going to add trampoline exercises to your daily routine," said one of the coaches. "I know some of you already do tramp exercises, but watch Curt Bryant, here from the gymnastics squad, do a few moves."

Angela later learned that Curt Bryant was a member of the gymnastics team who worked on the trampoline regularly to build up his legs.

Everyone watched attentively as Curt did a series of basic bounces, turns, and flips. Then one of the coaches pointed out some of the dangers of trampolines. They had a lot more spring than a diving board.

Angela spent the morning practicing on the trampoline, and asking Curt Bryant a lot of questions. The apparatus was completely new to her.

"Do you train on this thing at your college, Curt?" she asked.

"Only recently," he answered. "We just got a tramp. My college is small and can't afford much equipment."

"I guess you really had a fight on your hands, making the Olympic team from a small school."

"I haven't made it, yet. I'm only an outside shot for an alternate's position," said Curt.

"Did your high school have a team?" persisted Angela.

"No, no." He laughed. "I went to a small high school, way out in the mountain country. I learned gymnastics at home, part of my . . . my therapy."

Angela didn't pursue the matter then, but her conversation with Curt continued when he turned up in the cafeteria with his tray and there happened to be an empty seat at Angela's table. Kathy Rawls suddenly remembered she had to meet with her sisters, Dorothy and Evelyn, who were training with her in freestyle events.

"See you at the next workout," said Kathy leaving the dining hall.

"Curt," Angela began hesitantly, "you said something about 'therapy' this morning."

"I had polio when I was seven," Curt said. "My right leg was so skinny it looked like a stick, and my left leg would barely move. My family practically turned the house into a gym. We all worked together on my therapy—massage and exercise around the clock. And I made a sort of comeback."

"Curt!" cried Angela impulsively. "You mean just like Ray Ewry, and sort of like Glenn Cunningham?"

"Not 'sort of,'" Curt laughed. "Glen encouraged me a lot. He helped me vow to overcome, to try, and not to feel sorry for myself. He even came to see me once. He's here now, you know. He's got quite a race on his hands in Berlin. A New Zealand med student, Jack Lovelock, is a dark horse in the 1500-meter run."

So Curt knew Glenn Cunningham! Not just knew him,

Olympic Training Camp

but shared his struggle to make a damaged body become an athlete's temple.

"Curt, I come from Sandusky, a little town in Ohio. I'm sure you never heard of it," said Angela. "Well, it was a pretty big thing when a girl like me made the Olympic team, and my teachers had me read up on the Olympics and give special reports for my homework assignments. Have you ever met Ray Ewry? Have you heard of Eric Liddell?"

"I haven't met Ray Ewry," said Curt, "but they say he's an engineer or something here in New York, so maybe we could see him. I don't know very much at all about Eric Liddell, but one of your teammates told me a secret. He's your hero, isn't he, Angela?"

"He's more than a hero," said Angela. "You're going to think I'm soupy, just like a girl, or something. . . ."

"Try me," Curt said quietly.

"Things were hard for me, nothing like what you've had to go through, Curt, but I had no way to train and no one to help me at home. Eric Liddell showed me a way to believe, a way to aim at being a champion. Not just in swimming and diving, but in life, too. Do I make sense, Curt?"

"Angela, I should be fair with you," he answered. "I know about your quest for the incorruptible crown. I know who you are. I asked Coach to let me demonstrate the trampoline in the gym this morning so I could meet you where you could see how I am. And now I'm the one who feels foolish."

"You know about me, Curt?" asked Angela. "You arranged things to meet me?"

"Yes, I did, and that's not all," he said gently. "My father has been promoted with the coal company, and he's being transferred to Sandusky this summer. We're going to live there. I'm transferring to Ohio State as a sophomore in September."

Angela stared at her food. Curt wondered if he had said too much, too fast. He looked down. Then, their eyes slowly rose from their plates and met across the table. They both burst out laughing.

"I thought you'd make up an excuse to leave with Kathy Rawls if you knew that I rigged our 'chance' meeting," Curt explained.

Angela laughed. "And I thought you'd go sit at another table with some of the college girls when you found out I was a tenth-grader from a little town."

"Well, in a few minutes we are supposed to have a team meeting," said Curt, "but no tricks this time. I'd like to see you this evening, Angela. Could you come down to the rec hall?"

"Yes," answered Angela, "I'll come down. I'd like that. But don't be surprised if one of the other girls comes with me. We're supposed to stay together. You know, young girl in the big city, Olympic image, and all that stuff."

As Curt left for his meeting, Angela noticed that he did have a stiff gait, favoring his right leg.

Angela's afternoon consisted of backstroke laps and sprints. Since backstroke appeared to be the U.S. team's strength, "Sonny" Keifer and Barbara Eastman were the acknowledged team leaders. Both held the current world records. Eastman and Keifer were full of help and encouragement for their teammates. Angela found out that Barbara was fun, not awesome. And although at the AAU meet in Chicago Sonny had seemed

Olympic Training Camp

like a young god, he really was just a friendly eighteen-year-old high school boy.

Everywhere Barbara Eastman went, the press followed her. She was colorful. She was a true champion. She had married a well-known show business personality. Occasionally, Barbara would remind Angela, Alice Bridges, and Edith Motridge that she, Eastman, expected to take the gold medal in Berlin, but it was all part of the constant competitive banter. Angela enjoyed being around her because Barbara seemed to know everyone!

That evening, Angela and Alice Bridges went to the rec hall, where they chatted with Curt and a young rifle shooter who went to college with Curt. Their conversation was light and fun, comparing team experiences and hopes for success in Berlin.

The Olympic training camp routine suited Angela well. She thrived in this environment which valued her dogged persistence. Free of painful surprises, family problems, and petty jealousies among hometown people, she immersed herself in this dream world of great athletes. No one was asking her now if she was a cheerleader.

As the days whirled by, Angie grew to really appreciate letters from home. One letter from her father had especially pleased her. In his characteristic poor grammar he wrote:

> Dearest Angie,
> By now you're in the big city, working out with all the big time athletes. I wish we could have given you all that here at home.

> The house isn't the same with you gone. Your high school friends, they done something real nice for me. There's a boy, president of the class that just graduated, well he came by with your friend Mary. Seems that the class of 1936 made a present for you.
>
> One of them comes by every day to look in on me. Sometimes they just talk, some of them even cuts the grass out front. They keep asking about you. I read them a line or two from your letters, but of course I don't let them in on the private stuff you tell me.

(Angela made a mental note not to write anything private in her letters. Heaven only knew what he left lying around the house, and who would come snooping around and tell what they read!)

> Coach Miller and Sue call most days, and we share your letters. We all got a big kick out of the ladies on the train, that thought you were a cheerleader or something. I miss you, baby, take care of yourself.
>   Love,
>   Father

So the Class of 1936 had appreciated her attempt to keep graduation strictly for them! Angela felt very close to her high school friends—especially close, because they were helping her at home, the part of her life that had always been the most difficult to handle.

Soon it was July third, the anniversary of Angela's big win at the Battery Park Open Swimming Meet. Only one year before she had been a skinny high school girl, sneaking practice sessions and beating boys in races in Sandusky Bay.

But now the Olympic Committee had arranged a bus tour and weekend stay in New York City. As Angela

Olympic Training Camp

boarded the tour bus, she was delighted to find that Curt Bryant had saved a place for her next to him.

"How are the time trials going, Angie?" he asked. "Do you think you might be able to beat Barbara Eastman?"

"I don't know. Coach says I'm peaking," she replied. "But Curt, what about you? Have the gym coaches made the final team selection yet?" Angela felt embarrassed that Curt was asking about her progress while he faced the all-important question of whether he made the squad or would be sent home.

"Oh, that," said Curt, laughing a little. "What if I told you—" He paused dramatically, "—that I get to go to Berlin! The list just came out. I made the last reserve slot!"

"Oh, Curt!" said Angela, impulsively kissing his cheek.

"Wow!" said a wrestler in the seat behind them. "I just won the gold medal and inherited my grandfather's fortune. What do I get?"

Angela peered through the crack between the seats and blushed. "Congratulations, sir, twice," she laughed. Turning back she said, "Oh, Curt! I'm so happy for you, and for me. We'll be together in Berlin."

As Angela and Curt toured the nation's greatest city, they laughed at silly questions like, "Who's buried in Grant's Tomb?" and "Where does the Brooklyn Bridge go?" She wasn't homesick at all.

On the 4th of July, when Angie returned to the training camp, she found a money order, sent by Miss Foster with instructions to make several phone calls home. Angela had never made a long distance call. She was thrilled to hear her father, the Millers, and eventually, Miss Foster talking to her.

135

A LADY, A CHAMPION

After the 4th of July weekend, the entire U.S. Olympic team trained in earnest. On July 15, all 383 athletes (with the exception of a few who were already in Europe) would sail on the SS *Manhattan*, an American luxury liner. Although there was a swimming pool on board, shipboard workouts could never equal those at training camp. For the final week and a half Angela pushed herself hard, in both swimming and diving. As sailing date approached, she felt ready.

On July 14th, the athletes' training routine came to an end. Moving men came to the dormitory for the trunks and heavier luggage. The athletes spent much of their time dealing with Customs officials, verifying shot records, and dodging the ever-present photographers and newspaper reporters.

One woman reporter, who was irritated at not being able to isolate Barbara Eastman for a big interview, stopped Angela. "Angela, is it true you can beat Eastman now?"

"I don't know," Angie replied, "but I'll do my best in Berlin."

"What about your romance with Sonny Keifer?" persisted the woman, reaching for any kind of story. "You were with him in Chicago at the AAU's, you're both from the Midwest, and you're both of German background."

"Sonny—Adolph—is a wonderful athlete," said Angela, "but the only romance I have time for is my romance with the water and the diving board."

Fortunately, Angela did not see the tabloid the next day, quoting Angela as saying that she could whip Eastman now or any time, and fabricating lurid details about her nonexistent travels through the Midwest with Adolph Keifer. Angela knew nothing about the cruelties

Olympic Training Camp

that could be dealt out by the irresponsible element of the press.

On July 15, the U.S. Olympic teams' preparations for departure were tumultuous. Angela and her teammates heard rumors of how everyone was furious over Hitler's dislike of Jewish and Negro athletes, how the athletes were angry over the personal conduct rules, how Spain planned to boycott the Olympics, and more. In reality, these matters scarcely touched the athletes. While a few had been to previous Games or world matches and knew of the show business atmosphere which surrounds the Olympic team, most of them were from middle class families and lived relatively sheltered lives.

Angela was tired on sailing day. She had stayed up very late into the night writing her final letters and postcards home. Cautiously, she told Mary Zimmerman and Sue Miller a little about Curt Bryant. Painful memories of her experience with Ted Gunter made her fearful of any new relationship. She greatly missed Sue's guidance, yet she feared confiding in any of her teammates.

When boarding time arrived, Angela dressed in her neat white skirt and blue blazer with the U.S. Olympic team emblem, joined the long line of superb athletes who marched up the SS *Manhattan's* gangplank.

Heavy Movietone News cameras covered the event. Barbara Eastman was the center of attention, but the press highlighted all fifteen members of the attractive U.S. swimming and diving squads.

Once on board, each athlete went immediately to his or her assigned stateroom. In a daze, Angela followed the guide through the long passageways to the third class cabins which were to be the home of the U.S. Olympic team for the next two weeks. Quickly tossing her purse onto her bed, Angela ran back to the deck for a place at the rail, crowding in between Alice Bridges and Edith Motridge.

Angela looked all around her, not wanting to miss a single detail.

While one band played loudly on the dock, another band made their music somewhere on the ship. Stubby boats from the New York City Fire Department shot long streams of water into the air. Yachts passed by with cheering people at the rails. When the bands began to play "The Star Spangled Banner," the athletes put their hands over their hearts and stood proudly at attention. At the end of the song the *Manhattan* blasted her steam whistle, and the athletes leaped and cheered, their hearts pounding.

Huge ship's cables were thrown off of cleats that looked bigger than a crouching sailor. Great sloshing eddies of dirty-looking water swirled furiously as the ship slowly eased away from the pier. Assisting tugboats tooted their whistles in celebration.

"Edith," shouted Angela through the din, "I remember movies of old Olympic Games when I was in the sixth grade. We watched but I never dreamed it was like this."

"I know," yelled Edith. "They showed the famous athletes lined up at the rail waving. They don't show you their eardrums getting blasted out!"

A strong wave of patriotism swept throught the athletes as they sailed past the Statue of Liberty. Angela had never felt so proud to be an American. *This*, she thought, *must be how Father felt in 1918 or early*

Olympic Training Camp

1919, when he was brought home on a shipload of war-wounded. He said that bands played while crowds cheered at the dockside. How proud father must have felt, passing the Statue of Liberty, coming home to America.

Once clear of the harbor, the ship began to pitch and roll. By dinnertime the athletes had discovered that seasickness is no respecter of persons, even Olympic stars.

After dinner, those who felt well enough attended a pep talk and lecture by senior members of the U.S. Olympic Committee. Regular training would continue. Meal schedules would be followed. Athletes would remain in the third class accommodations out of respect for team training rules and to build esprit de corps.

Many of the athletes complained about the last part. A few of them had spouses staying in fancier staterooms aboard ship. But Angela noticed that most of the real champions did not oppose the rules, agreeing that team togetherness and discipline were central to the business of winning.

When the workouts began, the swimmers discovered that the pool water rolled back and forth with the motion of the ship. Since the pool was short, they tried swimming laps, in continuous circles, and relays. Using the pool at all hours of the day and night, the swimmers began to build a deeper sense of camaraderie.

Each evening there was some type of social event in the lounge or ballroom. The coaches were well aware that their charges were high-spirited young people who could not be sent to their rooms as soon as workouts ended.

One night, when there was a dance in the ballroom,

Curt Bryant walked up to Angela and tapped her on the shoulder. "Mr. Bryant would be pleased," he said, "if Miss Angela Weber would honor me with a dance."

"Miss Weber notices," said Angela with a smile, "that your name is right here on her dance card." She slid easily into his arms, feeling very happy, very close, and very hopeful. The orchestra kept them alternately slow-dancing and jumping to the latest swing tunes.

"Is going to the Games what you expected?" Curt asked.

"Not exactly," Angela replied. "I thought there would be big moral issues and dramatic stuff to deal with, like some of the things I read about for my school report."

"Angie," said Curt, "I think before this trip is over, you will get your share of big moral issues and drama. Many of us had to climb over many mountains to get here. For me, just being here is a miracle, and I probably won't even compete."

"I guess you're right," said Angie. "I guess I expected to see Jesse Owens racing around the decks, giving statements about being a success."

"Maybe he will, Angie," Curt said, grinning. "Maybe Angela Weber will do something before the Games are over that the kids in school will give reports about for years to come." He paused and his voice softened. "For now, I'm thanking God that we met, even if I did have to help the situation out a little back there in New York."

In two more days, the SS *Manhattan* would pull in at Cherbourg, France, where moral issues indeed would surface. For now, Angela loved the routine and Curt Bryant's attentiveness.

EIGHT
The XIth Olympiad

On Thursday, July 23rd, the SS *Mannhattan* docked in Cherbourg. Angela thought her father had mentioned sailing from there in the Great War, so she watched closely for details to put into a letter.

The French press was really excited because Barbara Eastman had been suspended from the swimming team for refusing to honor the training rules. Since Angela was Barbara's closest rival, she knew that anything she said could be taken in the wrong way. She decided to say nothing at all.

Some of the athletes wanted to sign a petition to embarrass the U.S. Olympic Committee, but Angela spent the next several hours moving around the ship to avoid the press. Then she slipped quickly ashore for postcards, again successfully eluding reporters.

When she returned, one of the woman gymnasts stopped her. "Weber," she said, "you'd better say something to the press. If you don't, they'll make up something anyway."

Angela wanted no bad sportsmanship attributed to her name. Actually, she had been looking forward to a head-to-head competition with Barbara Eastman and Rie Mastenbroek of the Netherlands. But as the SS *Manhattan* pulled away from the pier, Angela had successfully avoided all press interviews. Jesse Owens occupied much of the reporters' time, and of course, Barbara Eastman gave almost continuous interviews.

The ship headed up the English Channel into the rougher cooler waters of the North Sea. Now Angela was passing through an ocean where her father had never been. As she stood by the rail, Barbara Eastman approached.

"Angela, I want to talk to you," said Barbara calmly. "I'll admit I'm mad, and I've made some strong statements to the French press. But they're going to quote me as saying that I will take on the winner in Berlin and beat her easily. That's just press hype, you know. The truth is, I want you and Alice and Edith to win for America. And you have the best chance, Angie. I'll be pulling for you."

"Thanks, Barbara," said Angela. "The same goes for me about the press. I've said nothing at all, but they'll probably claim that I said I could have beaten you anyway. Who knows? Maybe we'll meet in the water at the national AAU's next year."

Barbara looked at Angela quizzically. "I thought you were a naive girl from a little town, Angela. I underestimated you. You're a champ, and also a lady."

Angela blushed. "I wish you the best, Barbara," she said simply. "You're a great person, and a friend."

The XIth Olympiad

Workouts continued their intensity aboard ship as the team got ready for docking in Hamburg, Germany. It was a gala welcome, not the same as their send-off in New York, but impressive. German naval vessels vied with merchant and passenger ships for space in the harbor.

The task of moving the Olympic team from the SS *Manhattan*, through the German Customs station, and on to the train was handled efficiently. The German railway system sped the impressed athletes through the beautiful countryside at an incredibly high rate of speed. Arriving in Berlin, the American veterans of the Los Angeles Games strongly approved of the Olympic village accommodations. "Much finer than what we had for the Xth Olympiad," they said.

During Angela's first night in the international commmunity of athletes, she walked around, taking in the sights and trying to identify the many foreign languages she heard around her.

On August 1, all the athletes from around the world rehearsed the opening ceremony. The German government had revived the custom of having the Olympic flame brought from Athens. Relay runners carried the torch on a long, zig-zag journey through the countries of Southern Europe, and finally to Berlin.

When the actual opening ceremony began, long lines of athletes stood outside the stadium listening to the roar of the crowd, which was watching a highly militarized show. Angela grinned to herself. She remembered Miss Foster's description of German band music, "Oom-pah-pah, Oom-pah-pah, as if they're all hooting out their noses."

Soon it was time to enter the stadium. Unit after unit

of neatly uniformed athletes, all in their national colors, marched through the tunnel and on around the field, creating the most elaborate and imaginative pageantry ever displayed in the modern Games.

Angela felt lost and nervous as she stood on the huge field in the middle of the U.S. team, and looked around the stadium at the enormous crowd. Chancellor Adolph Hitler proclaimed the opening of the XIth Olympiad, and a German athlete recited the athletes' oath in a stern, but moving voice. A runner carried the torch from Athens the last few meters and ignited the huge column of flame that would remain lit throughout the two weeks. Spiridon Louis, the Marathon champ from the 1896 Games, passed the olive branch of peace, re-enacting an ancient tradition. Flocks of doves were released, bands played, dancers performed, and flags and bunting moved gently on the soft summer breeze.

Once the teams got down to business, Angela had seven days to master the three-meter board in the beautiful, gleaming natatorium. She had qualifying heats for the first week, but her backstroke finals were well into the second week of the Games. She wouldn't have much free time.

Curt Bryant sent word to Angela that the gymnastics coaches were making pretty strong demands on their athletes' time, too, so he would have little time for sightseeing.

The first night of the Games, Angela spent two hours reading her mail. Some of the letters that had missed her earlier, caught up with her in Berlin, and she had a thick packet of letters from home to read.

Mary Zimmerman reported that she was now dating

The XIth Olympiad

Art Glover, Angela's old boyfriend. She said she hoped Angela wouldn't mind, and she mentioned that Mr. Weber thought it was kind of nice.

Father wanted to know if Angela had seen any men walking around wearing war medals, or with missing limbs, or anything else that would remind her of the Great War. Angela didn't know how to tell Father that the only military things she had seen were the Hitler Youth at the opening ceremony, and the guards in the Olympic village.

Miss Amanda Foster hoped that the elms along the *Unter-den Linden* were still as lovely in the summer. She also hoped that the Germans were providing some fine music, not just the kind that went "Oom-pah-pah, Oom-pah-pah." Angela stared in embarrassment at the large money order Miss Foster had tucked into her letter, complete with instructions on how to convert it into marks, where to shop for some fine clothes, and how to get them through Customs.

Coach Miller and Sue sent several thick letters with clippings about the U.S. Olympic team. Coach, in particular, praised Angela for the way she had handled the press. The Sandusky newspaper had printed a special editorial, telling how the girl who had been subjected to bad sportsmanship at Battery Park just a year before was now giving lessons to the Europeans about how to act when a famous rival is kicked off the team.

Why, oh why, Angela wondered, *can't people spend their time thinking about how I swim, about my flip turns, about sports?*

On Monday, August 3, Angela was resting after a strenuous workout when she received a message that she had a visitor. When she went down to the recreation lounge of the women's dorm, she was delighted to find Curt waiting for her.

"Hi," he said. "When is your first heat?"

"In three days," Angela replied. "I've had a great time getting to know Rie Mastenbroek. Her English is a lot better than my Dutch."

"Well, I'm glad you're friends with her, even if she is the main competition," said Curt.

"Do you have a chance of competing?" Angela asked.

"I do," he replied, "but it's a little bit like the way you don't have to swim against Barbara Eastman. One of our best gymnasts has a shoulder separation. It gives me a shot on the flying rings, but it hurts our team a lot."

"You know, Curt, when athletics first opened up to me, I thought there would be some clear book of rules, like the Bible, that would tell right from wrong in all these things," said Angela. "But the more I get into it, the more complicated it gets, and the harder it is to tell the good guys from the bad guys. The U.S. team would probably do better if Eastman and your injured gymnast were out there. You and I both want to compete and win, but we don't want to do it at somebody else's expense, or at the expense of our team's chances to win. It's all so complicated."

Three days later, on Thursday, there was nothing complicated about Angela's first 100-meter backstroke heat. Mastenbroek was not in that trial heat, but Alice Bridges was. Angela turned in her fastest time ever, 1:18.3, beating Alice by three meters. The friendly German crowd cheered, and many spilled over the restraining rail to convey their congratulations.

The XIth Olympiad

After the heat, Angela dressed quickly and met Curt outside the natatorium. Hurrying to the track stadium, they found two seats high up near the rim. They were just in time to see the finals of the 1500-meter race.

Angela didn't know much about running strategy, so when her hero Glenn Cunningham appeared to have a commanding lead, she stood and cheered ecstatically.

Curt was more cautious. "Look, Angie," he said, standing beside her. "Here comes Jack Lovelock, the dark horse!"

Angie focused her attention on the sandy-haired runner in a jet-black running suit. He was moving up fast as though he had it all planned. This was the New Zealand medical student who had taken running to new levels of physiological science.

The great Cunningham, who was also popular with the German crowd, did not have the kick necessary to hold off Lovelock. As the New Zealander broke the tape, Angela plopped down in her seat, dejected. It was so unfair! Cunningham deserved to win, and she wanted Curt to agree.

"Angie, I love Glenn Cunningham. I almost worshiped him when I was a little boy," said Curt. "But God doesn't pick out deserving people to win medals, not *human* medals. We show his power in running, swimming, and in all our living."

Angela knew that Glenn Cunningham himself would have said the same thing. As they walked back to the Olympic village, Angela was silent for several minutes. Finally she spoke.

"Curt, if I tell you something, do you promise you'll still be in my corner while I'm really under pressure?"

"Of course, Angie," said Curt. "You could tell me I'm

not as good looking as Sonny Keifer, and I'd still be crazy about you!"

Angie laughed. "I wanted to say something serious," she replied. "But you really are good for me."

"Well, speak, woman," commanded Curt. "I'm listening."

"OK, Curt, it's this," said Angela. "I got hurt last winter by a guy I really cared about. Ted Gunter was Sandusky's top athlete, and he seemed to understand my commitment to athletics. I thought he shared my standards, and—"

"And he got carried away one day with the incredibly beautiful Miss Weber, whose looks and personal standards are both a little higher than Mount Olympus. And she ended it, taking the pain in her wounded heart out on innocent national class swimmers at the AAU's in Chicago," said Curt.

"Oh, Curt, you—yes, that's about right. How do you know something before I even tell you?" she asked.

"Honestly, this time it was just a good guess. I *have* read all your clippings from the northern Ohio newspapers, though, and your fellow athletes speak highly of you. Angie," said Curt, "can I tell you something new?"

"Sure," she said.

"I care for you, but I'm in no hurry. Right now, I want to be important to you while you're under great pressure here. We'll see what happens later. Right now, you need someone to help you with your dreams, not someone to crowd you."

"Oh, Curt, I'm so glad you understand," said Angela, giving him a quick little kiss. "And now I have to get

The XIth Olympiad

back for a team meeting. Thanks for taking me to the 1500-meter race!"

Over the weekend, Angela spent more time with Rie Mastenbroek. Angela was amazed to find how much she had in common with the great Dutch star—age, background, personal standards, tremendous pressure. And they shared the dream of helping girls all over the world succeed in athletics.

On Monday, August 10, the natatorium was packed for the finals in the women's 100-meter freestyle event. Olive McKean and Kathy Rawls swam their best, but Rie Mastenbroek turned in a stupendous performance. The German crowd gave her a long standing ovation. Angela cheered proudly for her new friend, though she felt badly for Olive and Kathy, who took the disappointing sixth and seventh places, respectively.

The American women worked hard to keep team spirits high, but it was difficult. The next day was the final race in the 200-meter breaststroke. Iris Cummings and Dorothy Jane Schiller from the U.S. team swam valiantly but failed even to qualify for the finals. Consequently, Angela's performance on Wednesday in the three-meter springboard diving became the pressure point. Either the U.S. women's team would turn around and start winning, or they would be blown out of the Olympics.

On Tuesday night, a newspaper article taunted the American women. "What happened to the invincible California mermaids who were in Los Angeles?" the writer asked.

But Angela felt confident. Whenever the odds were against her, she again became the skinny girl at Battery

Park—withdrawn, a little angry, and athletically supercharged.

Kathy Rawls, of course, was the silver medalist from Los Angeles, and Dorothy Poynton-Hill was the world's top platform diver with much experience on the springboard, too. Both were confident, experienced divers, while Angela had only been competing at world competition levels for about eight months.

The five compulsory dives resulted in a very close point spread, with Kathy Rawls slightly ahead. The crowd quickly picked up the idea that it would probably be an American show. As they moved into the optionals, Angela's springy leg power and quick, whip-like openings from the pike position began to tell on the scoreboard. But the natatorium seemed chilly to Angela, and her muscles were tight.

On her next-to-last dive—the full gainer, pike position—Angela's ankle turned slightly on the takeoff. She held her body position, refusing to compromise the dive and her head missed the board by the thickness of a pencil. The crowd gasped. Angie held good position but entered the water at an outward angle. It cost her points. Going into the final dive, Kathy Rawls was 2.4 points ahead, and Dorothy was just three points behind.

Angie's selection for the last dive was the one-and-one-half backward somersault. Kathy's last dive was excellent, and Angela knew she would have to make a perfect score to win. This time, she felt the board carefully with her feet for any slippery or uneven spots. Finding none, she rose on her toes at the extreme end of the board, arms extended. The crowd hushed in anticipation.

The XIth Olympiad

To herself, Angie said, "Arms to your sides, take it well up, then drop it. Now, Angie. Now!"

She raised her arms, bent her knees slightly, then shot up and slightly backward. Her head dropped back, her arms opened out to both sides, and like the snap-blade of a jack-knife, her legs bent at the hips and came around above her. Back she dropped, spinning around a stationary point. Then at the perfect moment, she snapped straight again. A roar went up from the German crowd as she speared into the water, toes pointed straight up. The judges confirmed with their cards what the crowd had already decided.

Angela had won an Olympic gold medal. The final score was: Weber—89.27, Rawls—88.35, and Poynton-Hill—82.36. Pandemonium broke out on the American bench. The U.S. divers had swept all three medals. After hugging their teammates and jumping all around, the three divers pulled on their sweatsuits. Angela ripped off her bathing cap and ran her fingers through her hair, hoping it didn't look too tousled.

Security guards had to push the excited spectators back over the rail near the awards stand. Angela's feet seemed to hardly touch the floor as she mounted the stand with Kathy on her right and Dorothy on her left. The "Star Spangled Banner" had a hint of the "Oom-pah-pah, Oom-pah-pah" sound as the German band played, but it sounded heavenly to three victorious American women. Angela stood proudly, her shoulders erect, her hand over her heart, her eyes riveted on the American flag, as she sang the words to her national anthem. When the last note sounded, the crowd again roared its approval. Angela brushed big tears from her cheeks, then flashed a triumphant smile that made the front page of newspapers around the world. The American women were back in the Games!

When the victorious diving squad went to the Olympic Village, Angela needed to rest. Her final in the 100-meter backstroke was the next day. On the way to her room, Angie stopped at the check-in desk and found a note waiting for her.

> Angie,
> You are a true champion. Tonight and tomorrow, think only of your dreams. The rest of your crown will come when you need it.
>
> Fondly, Curt

There was nearly a half-day time differential between Berlin and Sandusky. When an all-night Cleveland radio station flashed the news about Angela's victory, people in Sandusky were heading out the door for their day's work.

Ted Gunter heard the news on his car radio. "Hey!" he shouted. "Hey, Angie did it!" There was no one but Ted in the car, for he was en route to a day of boating. Turning quickly, he drove to the little house where he used to pick Angela up for dates, when the two of them had something special.

"Mr. Weber! Mr. Weber! Angie did it!" he shouted, banging hard on the screen door.

Having a fairly good idea of what it was all about, Pete Weber wheeled his chair to the door.

"Hello, Ted. Good to see you," he said. "You say she did it?"

"The gold medal, Mr. Weber. The gold! For spring-

The XIth Olympiad

board diving. The United States swept the top three medals, and Angie won it!"

Pete Weber gripped the edge of the door. "Come in, son. Come in," he said.

"Not now, Mr. Weber. I've got to tell the town," said Ted. Scurrying around town, he posted a large, square, cardboard sign on the door of City Hall, on the main entrance to Sandusky High School, and at the Erie County Court House.

Angela Weber Won the Gold Medal in Diving Today!

Soon horns honked all over town, and church bells, which were customarily silent on a Wednesday morning in August, rang as though it were Christmas.

The Millers were so excited when they heard the news that they jumped up and down, hugging each other, and then immediately ran to the car to share the news with Miss Foster. They stayed with her all morning poring over Angela's letters for any scraps of information which might sweeten the victory.

Finally, Miss Foster observed that, with the time differential, Angela had already finished dinner and was probably resting for her backstroke final the next day.

In Berlin, Coach Kiphuth was analyzing the standings. The backstroke power of Angela and Sonny Keifer were essential to both the men's and women's teams. Rie Mastenbroek was practically winning the women's competition for her small country by herself. Her qualifying times in the freestyle events and the anchor leg of the freestyle relay seemed untouchable in the finals.

The next morning Angela felt confident. She knew

that Mastenbroek would improve upon her qualifying time in the final, but so would Angela. Alice Bridges had been improving steadily, too.

The crowd roared for the American women as they entered the natatorium, and again for the Netherlands team right behind them.

As the teams waited for the competition to start, Angela talked to Sonny Keifer. "Sonny," she said, "what do you think of the idea of staying close to the lane dividers? The Dutch girls were saying something about the surface current when you have a fast opponent in the next lane."

"America's best chance for a gold in this one," Sonny assured her, "is for Angela Weber to swim right down the center of her lane, keeping that good form that makes her so fast, and never forgetting that special edge she's carrying with her."

Angie smiled. "You were right about me in Chicago," she said, "and I think you're right again."

Angie would always treasure the fact that the fastest backstroker in history told her that her strongest features were also his. And it was true. Both Angela Weber and Sonny Keifer had the long arm reach, the high kick, the neat catch and release of the hands.

Yes, Angela was ready.

The announcer began calling the swimmers to their positions. "Rie Mastenbroek, lane 4, fastest qualifying time," he announced. Angela took her place on Rie's left, and the two of them were flanked by Alice Bridges and Edith Motridge. The crowd knew that any of the four could win as the finalists gripped the hand-holds, their bodies crouched in the water.

Barbara Eastman's disqualification had only height-

The XIth Olympiad

ened interest in this race. The fast qualifying times, two of them very close to Eastman's world record, clearly showed that these swimmers didn't consider themselves inferior substitutes.

After quieting the crowd, the starter called the swimmers up on the blocks. The competitors froze in place.

"Crack!"

Seven women fired backward in their lanes. Almost immediately, Angela and Rie Mastenbroek pulled one stroke in front of the others. In spite of the extremely fast pace, Angela concentrated upon holding her form. She couldn't afford any sloppiness.

At the halfway turn, Angela felt that her pace was very fast, but Mastenbroek didn't show any signs of slowing. Angie drove from the wall, straight into the center of her lane and picked up the armstroke. Suddenly, she thought Mastenbroek was coming toward her, crowding the lane divider.

Stay in the center, Rie. Stay in the center, she thought.

In front of the U.S. bench all of Angie's teammates were jumping up and down.

"Angie's got a thirty-eight second split!" shouted one of the coaches.

"Mastenbroek's on the lane divider," yelled Kathy Rawls. "What's she trying to do?"

"That's no accident," warned Olive McKean. "They've been talking all week about riding the divider, especially in the home stretch. They think it makes you go faster."

Fifteen meters out, everyone who could see the sweep of the second hand on the big wall clock could tell that both Rie and Angie were heading for a record.

Alice Bridges was only two or three strokes behind them.

Don't look over, girl. Don't look over, Angie told herself. *Pour it on. Go!*

Five strokes out from the wall, Angie saw what every swimmer dreams about. Mastenbroek dropped back, first inches, then a foot, until finally her head was opposite Angela's flutter kick.

Stretch, girl. Stretch for that wall, groaned Angela. And with an incredible last burst of speed, she touched the wall a full body length in front. Rie touched in two more strokes, and Alice Bridges finished just one stroke behind Rie. Leaning over the lane divider, Angie hugged Rie.

"You are the best, Angie," said Rie, in accented but clear English.

"In the backstroke, today," said Angie, out of breath, "but you're the greatest woman swimmer in the world."

Angie turned to the wall where there was a forest of hands and a blur of faces. She put her palms on the deck, scissored her legs, and did her neat kick-pull-and-rotate trick to exit the pool.

"Great job, champ," said Sonny Keifer, giving her a big hug. "It's a record. A big one!"

Angela's winning time of 1:16.2 was not just an Olympic record, but a new world record too! Now there could be no "what-ifs" from the press! No one would ever wonder if the United States could have taken the gold medal with different coaches, different swimmers, different team decisions. For Angela had done the most that an athlete can do. As the medalists approached the three-tiered awards stand, Rie Mastenbroek extended her hand. "Go up, champ," she said.

The XIth Olympiad

Angela stepped quickly to the top level, with Rie on her right and Alice on her left. The chief judge approached, taking a gold medallion on a ribbon out of a small box which was held out for him. Angela leaned forward as the judge slipped the ribbon over her head. Straightening up, Angie shook out her hair and stood proudly as the announcer read out her name and the new Olympic and world record time.

Then, as the American flag started up the pole, Angela felt the significance of what she had done. She was the first person in the world ever to win gold medals in both swimming and diving. Her victories had restored the U.S. women's swim team to first place, at a time most people said they were beaten.

Again, with tears streaming down her cheeks, Angela sang the words to the "Star Spangled Banner." The crowd loved it all—her smile, her pretty face and hair, even the tears. Angela was the darling of 25,000 people, most of them Germans.

At the end of the national anthem, Angela stepped down and walked directly over to Dorothy Poynton-Hill. "I hope success is catching around here," she said. "I'll be pulling for you this afternoon as if each one of your dives were my own."

After lunch, Angela sat on the bench with the divers for the platform finals. Dorothy Poynton-Hill had never performed better. Over and over, her polished form brought roars of approval from the friendly crowd. She started out her compulsory series in sharp form and improved with each dive.

When the final scores were announced, Dorothy was not only the gold medal winner, she was the greatest woman Olympic diver in history, and Angela was the first person to tell her so. Two platform golds in two consecutive Olympiads, and a silver and a bronze in the springboard were her proof! Velma Dunn came in less than half a point back in the platform diving to take the silver medal. It was another American women's sweep.

Later in the afternoon, the U.S. women medalists were brought into a small conference room for interviews with the press. Angela felt the German journalists were as articulate in English as the Americans, and less likely to stab the athletes with mean questions.

Angela and Dorothy, of course, received most of the attention. The reporters asked Angela many questions about her training, her technique, but little about personal matters. She enjoyed telling how the leg spring exercises she did to enhance her diving were helpful in the pushoffs in swimming, although they sometimes caused leg cramps in the straightaway.

As the interview ended, the door opened and three men in suits entered. Two were from the U.S. Olympic Committee and one was with the U.S. diplomatic service in Berlin.

"These must be the American officials with an invitation for the beautiful American divers," said one of the journalists.

The three men called Angela and Dorothy aside to explain that they had received a very high level German invitation for them to attend a government function. Unfortunately, some of the leaders at the function would be emphasizing the superiority of blond Aryan athletes, and there was a potential for embarrassment.

Quickly, the officials explained to Dorothy and Angela the fine points of diplomatic protocol. If they refused the invitation, it could be considered an insult to

The XIth Olympiad

the German government. If they accepted, some Jewish and Negro Americans might take offense if they thought two American athletic champions were siding with the Germans against them. That's the way it might look.

"Has anyone here heard the story that's going around the Village about Jesse Owens and the long jump?" asked Angela.

"Yes," said Dorothy, "Jesse himself was telling it."

"You mean how the German athlete, Lutz Long, showed him the foul line in the qualifying jumps and kept him in the finals?" asked one of the officials.

"Yes, of course," said Angela. "It was a real act of sportsmanship. Jesse beat Lutz Long in the finals. If Lutz had kept his mouth shut, he might have won the gold medal for himself. And afterward, when Jesse won, Lutz shook his hand right there in front of the German leaders. Isn't that what the Olympics are supposed to be all about?"

The officials exchanged glances.

"What would you propose to do, Angela?" asked one of the Olympic officials.

Quickly, she took a sheet of paper off the table and fished for a pen in her purse. Writing out four or five lines, she handed the paper to Dorothy for approval.

"Mrs. Poynton-Hill and Miss Weber are pleased to accept your invitation to represent America's athletes of all races and creeds," read Dorothy. "They will be honored to join with German athletes who share this true Olympic ideal."

"Pretty sharp, Angie," said Dorothy.

"Can you have someone type it in the right form or something?" asked Angela. "That way, we're being polite, but we're telling them who we really represent."

"Angela," said the diplomatic corps officer, "when you're ready to retire from athletics, I hope you'll apply to the State Department. I get your point. Let us handle it verbally. We'll get your message across."

The little meeting broke up, and Angela went back to her room. Now she could shop. She could forget her diet, try some of the rich German food, even stay up too late. Now she would visit some of the places Miss Foster and her teachers wanted to hear about when she returned to Sandusky. Perhaps Curt could even go with her.

In Sandusky, Thursday, August 13, started ordinarily enough for Miss Amanda Foster. The night before, she had gone to bed, glowing with happiness over Angela's springboard victory. She couldn't be sure how the backstroke would come out, but she wasn't worried about Angela's ability.

Thursday morning, as Miss Foster drank her coffee and ate her Danish, she read all the stories in the area newspapers about the U.S. Olympic team. Suddenly, the phone rang.

"Miss Foster," said David Miller, "is your radio on?"

"No," she said. "Is there more news from Berlin?"

"Angela has won the 100-meter backstroke," Coach Miller almost shouted. "In world record time! She's the only person in history ever to win gold medals in both a swimming and a diving event."

Tears of joy filled Miss Foster's eyes. The double gold! What a nice sound that had.

"I wonder, Miss Foster," David Miller continued, "if

The XIth Olympiad

you would like to visit Mr. Weber with Sue and me this afternoon? The high school kids are over there now, and it's pandemonium!"

Just then there was a giant blast from the usually silent steam whistle at the paper box factory, and Miss Foster began to realize a little of the pandemonium that was spreading through Sandusky.

"Around two," she said. "Can you pick me up then?"

"We'll be there," said Coach Miller.

Far away in Berlin, Angela was starting to comprehend what was happening. Up to now, she had just been trying to do her best and not think much about other things. But now she wanted to share her triumph with the right person. Somehow Curt Bryant seemed to be the one.

"Hi, Angie, you did it all!" was his greeting to her. "How about a little sightseeing? I don't have to be at the gym until tomorrow afternoon at two."

"I'd love to go sightseeing, Curt," she said, "but be sure to tell me when you do the flying rings event so I can watch you," she said.

"Well, actually I already had my shot," Curt replied sheepishly. "I didn't win any medals, but at least I got out on the floor."

"Oh, Curt!" Angela frowned. "You said it was this evening or tomorrow, and I've missed seeing you now!" Again, Curt seemed to be standing in her shadow, and she didn't like that.

Curt laughed. "There was a schedule change on short notice, and you couldn't have made it in time anyway," he said. "Feel good for me, Angie. I feel good. I made the team, and I got to wear this U.S. Olympic team emblem while I competed out there on the floor. For me, that's a crown to wear, see?"

Angela hugged Curt. "Here's joy in it, Curt," she said. "You're my idea of a real athlete, a real man."

In an effort to change the subject, Curt pulled out a map of the city and asked Angie what she most wanted to see. For the next four hours, they saw the sights of late afternoon and early evening in Berlin.

Just after lunch in Sandusky, Art Glover and Mary Zimmerman arrived at Angela's house to share the big moment with Mr. Weber. High school kids were everywhere, but Mr. Weber wasn't in the house.

"He's out on the back porch, and actin' strangely today," said the housekeeper. "Important people, people who pay certain other people's wages, are comin' over and I've got the dishes to clean up."

Art and Mary slipped out onto the little back stoop. Mr. Weber wasn't there either, although several high schoolers had seen him in the crowd.

"Mrs. Hudson," said Mary to Angela's motherly next-door neighbor, "have you seen Mr. Weber?"

Mrs. Hudson put two clothespins in her mouth, thought for a minute, then hung up a shirt.

"No, he was puttering around there a while ago, after the big news came in about Angie," said the kindly woman. "Come to think of it, he went out the path towards the front yard. Did my heart good to see him walkin', all springy, even with that cane of his."

Mary and Art darted back inside. "Mr. Weber's gone somewhere! He never goes anywhere unless someone with a car takes him."

The XIth Olympiad

The housekeeper's face clouded with worry. "Ride around on your bikes and look for him," she snapped. "And hurry or I'll be blamed. Miss Foster is coming over to see him, and the newspaper man is on the way, too."

As more of Angela's high school friends came by, they were all commissioned to try to find Mr. Weber.

"Hey, look here," said Art. "There's a note pinned to this corkboard."

Inside the big oval ring of medals, where the nursing cap badge and the Silver Star hung together, was a scrap of paper. On it, Mr. Weber had scrawled: Put them here, baby. You honor your mother and father.

"Oh," cried Mary, "that's a special vow Angie made to him."

The housekeeper wasted no more time and called the Millers. Coach Miller immediately phoned the Sandusky Police Department, but they could do very little.

"It's not against the law for Mr. Weber to be around town," said the desk sergeant. "Does anyone know that he's in trouble? Seems like if he can walk away from the house, he must be able to get along. Where's the harm?"

Reluctantly, the sergeant agreed that he'd order his downtown sector patrol cars to be on the lookout for a man with a cane. By dinnertime, Mr. Weber was not back, and many people were worried.

The Sandusky Police Department, not wanting to do anything that would embarrass Angela's hour of glory around town, initiated a quiet search in bars and restaurants that Weber had frequented years before.

While Miss Foster, the Millers, and others were worrying about Mr. Weber's whereabouts, Angela was fast asleep. She had had a fun evening with Curt.

A LADY, A CHAMPION

Next morning, in the women's dorm, she received a whole pile of messages. After getting dressed and eating breakfast, she planned to join the swimming team at the natatorium. They all wanted to cheer Sonny Keifer home to victory in the men's 100-meter backstroke. And she couldn't miss cheering for the American foursome in the 4 x 100-meter freestyle relay.

Angela boarded the bus happily, chattering with swimmers, trying to help everyone get into a winning frame of mind.

As she stepped off the bus at the natatorium, Coach Kiphuth and an Olympic committee member approached her. "Angela, please join us in this office a minute," said Coach Kiphuth.

Supposing there must be some new information about the German government function that she and Dorothy were supposed to attend, Angela sat down, unconcerned. Then an elderly gentleman in a clerical collar joined them at the little conference table. Suddenly the mood changed.

"Angela, this gentleman is acting as chaplain for the Olympic team," said Coach Kiphuth.

"You have soared to the heights of athletic achievement, Angela," said the chaplain, "and they tell me your athletics is just part of a deep religious power in your life."

"Yes, that's true," said Angela.

"God calls you now to endure a tragedy, Angela," he continued.

Angela's heart pounded.

"I have here a very long cablegram," the clergyman said, "sent late last night from a Miss Amanda Foster in Sandusky, Ohio. It came to the U.S. Embassy during

The XIth Olympiad

the night and was brought straight here by messenger."

"Miss Foster sent a night cablegram?" asked Angela. "Why?"

"My dear girl, God has called your beloved father home," said the chaplain. "He died last night, full of joy over his daughter's achievements. Our deepest sympathy, Angela. We'll do anything that you wish."

Angela's breath came in short little gasps like at the end of a hard race. "How did he—Father—die?" she asked.

"Do you want to know, my dear?" asked the chaplain. "It's hard to hear. Your father was a war hero and also a troubled sick man, I'm told."

"How did Father die?" persisted Angela, her voice calm but insistent.

"Dear God, give me strength," said the chaplain. "You must brace yourself, Angela. Your father left home and went out to celebrate. I guess the whole town was out in the streets."

"And someone gave him some whiskey, didn't they?" asked Angela. "A sick man, who had people watching over him for me, to care for him while I was gone like Miss Foster promised—"

"Oh, yes, Angela. It's the worst you can imagine," said the chaplain. "He went somewhere called Water Street, to a bar, found some old friends. After dark, he wandered off from the group and walked along the docks. A fisherman found him by one of the piers, just after midnight, Angela. Oh, dear God," the chaplain's voice broke. "They found him in Sandusky Bay."

Angela peered through a haze at these three men. Her world was not just upside down. It had a knife, a red hot knife, stuck right down into the most vulnerable window of her soul.

"This is my crown, my gold crown that I set out to win," she said softly. "My mother died at my birth. My father drowned at the victory celebration over my Olympic medals. My parting prayer, Chaplain, in my living room as I held Father's hand, was—if I could win an Olympic medal, it would be to honor my father and my mother."

"It is cruel beyond human understanding, Angela," said the chaplain.

"It didn't all come out wrong," continued Angela, in a soft voice. "I won two medals, one for each of them, so I could honor them both. But, instead, I lost them both."

Angela stood up slowly. "I dedicated myself to freeing my life. We were so poor, and Father was always sick. But I found out I could swim and dive very well, and I learned in church about Eric Liddell—how he ran for God, how he gave up athletic glory after showing the world God's power in his body, all in order to win an incorruptible crown."

The chaplain looked at her, his face full of compassion.

"What kind of incorruptible crown is it, Chaplain," asked Angela, "that honors both my mother and my father by taking away their lives? What kind of crown is that, Chaplain?"

NINE
Angela's Crown

"I have two requests, Coach Kiphuth," said Angela. "I want to be with the team now, while Sonny and the freestyle relay swim their finals. Don't tell them anything. Let me do it after the races."

"That's a courageous thing. Of course you can," said Coach Kiphuth. "What else, Angela?"

"I want the chaplain to send a cable—I have money to pay for it—to Reverend Eric Liddell in China. Send it now, please. I'll write out the message," said Angela.

On a sheet of paper, Angela wrote:

> To: Rev. Eric Liddell
> Tientsin Anglo Chinese College
> Tientsin, China
>
> My incorruptible crown: two Olympic Golds, two innocent parents dead. Why does God let the innocent

167

suffer? I only sought to honor him by honoring my parents.

> Angela Weber
> U.S. Olympic Team
> Berlin, August 4, 1936

"I will send it now, Angela," said the chaplain.

Angela walked out of the conference room, into the huge natatorium. Mustering a smile, she made up a little tale, letting Dorothy Poynton-Hill think there was some problem in the wording of their message to the German government about the invitation.

By cheering her teammates on, she thought she would be able to put some kind of meaning into the grief that filled her heart. Maybe Father wasn't much of a success, but he was brave. That day in 1918, when his body was torn up by German fire, he did not quit. He dragged two wounded Americans through a hail of bullets to safety.

Just before Sonny Keifer's race, Angela spoke to him. "Sonny," she said, "that center lane has a deep groove right in the middle of it. You get in there and win!" She flashed a huge smile.

Minutes later, Sonny Keifer stood on top of the award stand, his American teammate on his right. A stupendous new Olympic men's backstroke record flashed on the lighted scoreboard. Angie remembered the first time she had seen Keifer at the AAU Nationals. *How would he deal with the things she was feeling right now?* she wondered.

Most of the U.S. team skipped lunch, too excited to

Angela's Crown

eat. Angela slipped quickly back into the little office where the coaches did their business.

"Angela," said Coach Kiphuth, "there's another cablegram from Miss Foster. She's willing to pay your way home right now by airplane if you want it. The State Department checked the flight schedules. The earliest you could make it home is late Monday night, and that's if all the weather and plane connections are perfect."

"That must cost a fortune," said Angela slowly, "and they'll—Pastor Bob—the burial will probably be Sunday, the same day as the closing ceremonies, right Coach?"

"Yes, the funeral is scheduled for Sunday, according to the cable," answered Coach Kiphuth. "Look, Angie, I haven't been your coach for very long, but may I give you an old coach's opinion?"

"Of course," said Angela.

"Well, it's magnificent what you did this morning," he said. "And it's characteristic of you. Angela Weber doesn't pull her dive when she has a bad takeoff. She doesn't hide in the locker room when she faces a tragedy. Staying with this team to the end, going home with them—"

"Yes, go on," said Angela.

"It keeps you among people who love you, who share your dreams," said Coach. "And, most important, you honor your father's memory by courageously giving of yourself when most people would be sitting around feeling sorry for themselves."

"Yes," said Angela, "I see." She blinked back tears.

"And," finished Coach Kiphuth, "it honors you, Angela. I'm a swimming coach, not a minister, but I think a strong finish in this awful tragedy you've had, a strong finish in this hardest of all races may just win you your crown. Isn't that what you're really after, Angela?"

"It's true," whispered Angela. "It's true. Help me, Coach Kiphuth. Help me finish this race like a champion."

That afternoon, as Angela and her teammates cheered, the U.S. women's 4 x 100-meter freestyle relay team won the bronze medal, while Rie Mastenbroek led the Dutch team to a record-breaking gold.

Friday night, Angela sat quietly with Curt in the lounge, telling him how her world had seemed to fall in when she was finally at the top. She sounded more bitter now. Curt was wise enough to see that her grief must come out, and that Angela was turning to him in her need.

On Saturday, Curt sat with the U.S. swim team as they rooted Lenore Wingard Kight to a bronze medal in the 400-meter freestyle. Rie Mastenbroek put another new record on the board, bringing her total medals to three gold in the freestyle events and a silver medal in the backstroke.

Angela posed for a photograph with Rie and told the reporter that Rie was the world's greatest woman swimmer.

After the last event, Coach Kiphuth assembled his two teams to congratulate them and to thank them for their dedication. Although this was the U.S. swimming and diving team's narrowest Olympic victory since they established supremacy in 1920, the coach reminded

Angela's Crown

them that it still was a sweet victory. "The world is in turmoil," Coach Kiphuth told them, "but the 1940 Olympic Games are scheduled for Japan, and I hope many of you will return."

After the coach finished his speech, Kathy Rawls and Sonny Keifer spoke privately to individual team members about Angela's tragedy. They were all deeply moved by her decision to remain with the team, and her determination to keep the news secret to avoid upsetting the team's performance. There was not a dry eye anywhere in the two locker rooms as the U.S. swimmers and divers packed their gear to leave.

Rie Mastenbroek sat quietly with Angela for several minutes, sharing their common grief and courage. The bonds of a life-long friendship would survive war, triumph, and personal adversity for both women.

Saturday night when Angela and Dorothy were to attend the big German government affair, the event was mysteriously cancelled. Instead, the two joined the entire U.S. Olympic team at a lovely banquet sponsored by an appreciative American overseas community in Berlin.

Sunday morning, as Angela was dressing to attend an early chapel service, a cablegram arrived from China. She started to open it, then put it into her purse and went out to the lounge where Curt was waiting.

"I have a cable from China," she said, showing him the yellow envelope.

"Do you want to open it alone?" asked Curt.

"No, I want you to sit right there, and we'll read it together," she said, tearing the envelope gently along the seal.

TO: Miss Angela Weber, Champion
   USA Team, Olympic Village
   Berlin, Germany

Angela: Your medals show God's power at work in athletics. Your crown shows God's power in your heart. Seek his love now in your grief, and the incorruptible crown will be your life.

> Eric Liddell
> Tientsin Anglo Chinese College
> Tientsin, China

"Angela," said Curt, "I didn't know anything about Eric Liddell until I read a quote in the newspaper where you mentioned him. But evidently the man is a true champion and a true man of God."

That afternoon, at the closing ceremonies, there were many emotional moments among the athletes from around the world.

How could people from different countries think of killing each other? Angela wondered. She watched Jesse Owens shake hands with Lutz Long. Glenn Cunningham bent his head in conversation with Jack Lovelock! Angie found Rie Mastenbroek and they hugged like two girls who had grown up in the same family.

"No," Angela told Curt later, "people could not make war anymore."

Again, her father's death took on meaning. He sacrificed so much in the Great War to win peace. Didn't the governments of the world owe him a look at what was happening right there among the Olympic athletes? She remembered Juliet's lament from her

Angela's Crown

Shakespeare readings in Miss Hartung's English class. "Take him," Juliet said, "and cut him out in little stars, and he shall make the face of Heaven so fine. . . ."

Sunday night the U.S. team's luggage was picked up, swollen with souvenirs and other purchases from the little shops of Berlin. The scenic ride to Hamburg kept Angela peering out the window, not wanting to miss a thing. Then as she waited with Curt to board the ship, a messenger handed her a cablegram.

"How did these Germans ever find me?" Angela asked Curt. "Their efficiency is amazing!" she said, opening the cablegram.

> TO: Miss Angela Weber, U.S. Olympic Team
> Hamburg, Germany
>
> Angela. Funeral of Peter Weber today paid honor to his name. Pastor Bob Slayton eulogized his service to his country, his love for your mother, and his adoration of his daughter. Now she must come home to her crown. Love,
>
> Amanda Foster
> Sandusky, Ohio, USA
> August 16, 1936

"Angie, you should send a cablegram yourself," said Curt. "The people in Sandusky are going to want to honor you. But they won't be sure what to do because of your father's death. You should tell them how you want to be treated."

Monday night, Angela's return cablegram arrived in Sandusky.

TO: Miss Amanda Foster
    Sandusky, Ohio, USA

Miss Foster: Please ask Sandusky to honor the Olympic team when I arrive Wednesday, August 26, on the 9:30 A.M. train from New York. Father would not want tears. I want to honor Father. I know you will explain it right. Love to Coach and Sue, too.

                              Angela Weber
                              Hamburg, Germany
                              August 17, 1936

When Miss Foster read the cable, she smiled and called the mayor.

"A certain knight is riding home from battle on her horse," said Miss Foster. "Now here is what Sandusky is going to do. . . ."

When Angela and Curt boarded the passenger liner in Hamburg, it was the beginning of an unforgettable trip to New York. Angie talked Curt into joining her in the swimming pool, and they played like high-spirited children. Gone was the tension, the sense of great mission. Angela kept her grief to herself. During this cruise she wanted to enjoy being a beautiful girl on a luxury liner, surrounded by magnificent athletes who were her friends, and a handsome young man who cared for her more than he dared to admit.

Curt began teaching Angela some gymnastics, too. Angie borrowed an outfit from one of the woman gymnasts. She showed a great aptitude for the floor exercises and the flying dismounts, but the demands of the bars made her supple muscles ache. Most of all, Curt enjoyed seeing Angela laugh like a delighted child when she took an un-champion-like flop.

Each night the two danced and talked. Their relation-

Angela's Crown

ship had grown as they shared emotional mountaintops in Germany, but they needed time to relax, to be silly, to be young people falling in love. And Angela needed time to deal with her grief, to get her father's death into perspective.

When the ship docked in New York, huge crowds welcomed them with cheers and whistles. Fire boats pumped their water high in the air as bands played, flags waved, and fireworks boomed like cannons. When the Olympic team left the ship, there was great confusion as they tried to get all of their luggage through Customs. And the press—there was always confusion with the press.

"Is it true that you could beat Rie Mastenbroek of Holland, head-to-head?" "Are you going to swim off a grudge race against Barbara Eastman?" "Are you marrying Adolph Keifer during Labor Day weekend?" "Is it true that a drunken citizen killed your father while celebrating your winning the medals?"

Curt and Coach Kiphuth tried to shield her, but Angela, herself, handled the press. And moments later, when Jesse Owens came off the ship, the reporters all ran toward him, hoping to get a fresh comment before he was swept off for the tickertape parade which was about to begin.

When they finally cleared the pier, Curt's parents were waiting outside, having come to New York on business. Curt planned to drive home to Colorado with them. The family would move to Sandusky in October, although Curt had to be at Ohio State just after Labor Day.

Mr. and Mrs. Bryant offered Curt and Angela tickets to a play for the evening but Angela preferred that the four of them have dinner together.

"I want to get to know you while Curt is here with us," said Angela. "When you move to Sandusky, I'll be going to high school, and Curt will be in Columbus. We'll hardly ever see each other."

Mrs. Bryant smiled. "I'm afraid I'll have to correct you on one point, Angela," she said. "Curt has already ordered four season tickets to the Ohio State football games, and engaged his father and me to chauffeur and chaperone a certain lady Olympic star."

"I can hardly wait!" said Angie. "It's like a dream, Mrs. Bryant."

Angela enjoyed a lovely dinner in New York, with Curt and his parents, then got a room at the hotel where the Bryants were staying, and did some shopping with Mrs. Bryant the next day. They talked happily of plans for the Bryants' move to Sandusky. Curt seemed to assume that Angela was part of his future, but he never pushed her.

By mid afternoon on August 25, Angela was a little embarrassed at all the baggage the redcap was putting on the train for her. Standing on the lower step of the Pullman car, Angela hugged Mr. and Mrs. Bryant goodbye. Curt kissed Angie warmly, assuring her he would see her soon. Angela went to her seat, peering out the window and waving.

This time she had the seat to herself and she appreciated the restful quiet. At dinner, Angela sat with two college girls returning home to Toledo after a trip east. They recognized her immediately and asked for her autograph. When Angie told them the story of the two ladies who thought she might be a cheerleader with the

Angela's Crown

Olympic team, the girls laughed delightedly.

"Where will you go to college, Angie?" asked one girl.

"I don't know—maybe Ohio State," said Angela. "Someday, colleges will have competitive swimming teams for girls instead of just water ballet clubs."

"Will you model swimsuits and perform in the Aquacade, like Aileen Riggin?" asked the second girl. "I heard there's big money in it."

"Right now, I'm thinking of becoming a teacher for crippled and handicapped children," said Angela. "It's not that I couldn't use the money—goodness knows how poor I really am—but I've had this dream always, about what I could do for people."

As the train slipped around the last long curves east of Sandusky, the two girls from Toledo helped Angela get her things together. No one could have predicted the greeting as the train screeched to a stop, but Angela began to get the idea when she saw the sea of faces that extended way out beyond where the station platform began.

Poker-faced, the Pullman porter said, "Step careful, now, Miss." He took Angela's hand and guided her to the important little metal stool that he placed on the station platform.

When Angela's foot touched the stool, the National Guard Battery began firing a cannon salute.

Boom! The first cannon fired, and a band which Angela could not even see began playing the "Star Spangled Banner." The Mayor began to speak but Angela could not hear him. An announcer shouted something into a microphone. *Boom! Boom! Boom!* The cannons continued to fire as Angela made her way to a wooden platform mounted on the back of a truck. The platform was festooned with red, white, and blue crepe paper streamers. Huge banners down the sides of this impromtu chariot proclaimed: WELCOME, SANDUSKY'S OLYMPIC CHAMPION, ANGELA WEBER!

When the cannons finished, the band picked up a spirited march. Angela mounted the fancy platform on the truck, and the parade began. The enthusiasm lasted all the way down Hayes Avenue, through the downtown blocks, to the big, open park area around the Erie County Court House. People lined the streets, waving flags and calling out her name. When the music waned at times, the honking horns from the two-mile long motor cavalcade took up the slack. Over the din of horns, the factory whistles let out long blasts and bells rang in their steeples as Angela passed. Even the freighters in Sandusky Bay blasted their horns.

Finally, around 11:00 A.M., the mayor quieted the crowd and made his carefully rehearsed welcoming speech, which was largely written by Miss Foster. Then the mayor asked if Angela had a few words for Sandusky.

Angela stood before the microphone proudly. "When I was standing on the winner's box in Berlin, draped with the Olympic gold medals," she began, "I heard our national anthem, and I watched the American flag rise. Only then, could I understand what it means to be an athlete from our great country."

Wild cheering broke out, which lasted for several minutes.

"I guess," continued Angela, "that not every skinny little girl who swims at Battery Park can become a champion. But every boy and girl can try. Everyone is a

Angela's Crown

champion at something. I wanted to be on the Olympic team to prove something to myself, and to honor my mother and father."

The crowd hushed.

"Just over there," she said, pointing to a large bronze tablet on the courthouse lawn, "is a list of men from Sandusky who lost their lives in the Great War. And now my father has gone to join them, a hero of that war. I'd like to think that Sandusky honors Father today, as you have so kindly honored his daughter."

There was a moment's awkward silence, and then the cheering erupted again, wave upon wave, at a level that reached deeply into people's hearts. It was a moment that Sanduskians would never forget.

"As long as America stands up for what is right," Angela told the crowd, "as long as America sends out Olympic athletes like the men and women who just came back from Berlin with me, I know we are the greatest nation in the world!" She raised both arms over her head and clasped her hands. The summer breeze lightly blew her blonde hair, and as she stood on the decorated platform in her white skirt and blue Olympic blazer, hands clenched overhead, she made an unforgettable picture.

For a long time Angela stood waving at the crowd. This was a rally of joy, of welcome, of honor to a magnificent young girl, and it would live in her memory forever.

After the rally, Angela joined Coach Miller and Sue at Miss Foster's for lunch.

On the way, Sue spoke tenderly to Angela. "Your baggage, honey, is already over at our house," she said. "David and I hope you will come to live with us now."

Angela hugged Sue impulsively. "Oh, that would be wonderful, Sue," she said, fighting back the tears.

Miss Foster wanted to hold the Olympic medals. She squeezed the gleaming discs with her strong hands, turning them, and squinting at the engraving. "How incredibly beautiful they must have looked, hanging around your neck, Angela," she said. "On the platform in the park, I could really only see the ribbons crossed in front of you. These medals are just the thing for my lady knight to be bringing home."

Angela spent the rest of the day with the Millers and the telephone, unpacking, sorting, telling stories, and trying to identify the voices of those who called to wish her well.

The next day, Angela made a very important trip with the Millers, Pastor Bob, and Miss Foster to the courthouse.

"I have had my attorney work out some elegant-looking papers, Angela. I want to spare you, as you well deserve to be spared, having to sell your talent and beauty in order to finish your education. My attorney will explain it all to you, and then, if you accept, we will go into the judge's chambers to make it official," said Miss Foster.

Miss Foster had dedicated a part of her fortune to create a trust fund for Angela which produced both a monthly income and an additional allowance to pay for college, room and board, and travel, should she want to continue her athletic career. As a safeguard, Susan Miller would become Angela's legal guardian until Angie turned twenty-one.

"After all, Angela," said Miss Foster, "I hardly think

Angela's Crown

that Sue will stop you from buying a gorgeous new dress when you want it, but she could be very helpful if some lecherous old man tries to steal your trust fund."

The judge asked Angela if she had any questions.

"I'm very honored to have Miss Foster take such good care of me," Angela replied. "I guess my only question is, may I have permission to keep my parents' personal effects, and to maintain their graves?"

"Of course, Angela," the judge answered. "Now, Miss Weber," he said in a very businesslike tone, "we have a whole pile of papers for you to sign, legal papers that will give you the kind of future and dignity that you deserve. But first, do you think—," he grinned at her sheepishly, "that you could autograph this photograph that was in last night's paper with your speech in the park? See, my face just shows the least little bit, behind your arm there. . . ."

Everyone in the judge's chamber opened their mouths in amazement, then exchanged amused glances.

The traditional Labor Day festivities at Cedar Point Amusement Park became an Angela Weber Appreciation Day, sponsored jointly by the chamber of commerce and the Cedar Point Company.

Angela gave an exhibition of swimming and diving, wearing her Olympic bathing suit. Thousands agreed that she was the most tastefully attractive athlete they had ever seen, and Angie was delighted that her presence pepped up business for the area merchants.

Angela stayed in training for the 1940 Olympics during her junior and senior years of high school, and she defended her National AAU titles and records successfully.

She continued her friendship by mail with her American teammates and with Rie Mastenbroek in Holland. Many weekends she went to Columbus to see Curt after the Bryants moved to town. Both Miss Foster and the Millers thoroughly checked out the Bryants and decided that if Angela had to fall in love with someone, Curt would be very acceptable.

Curt majored in physical education and education management at Ohio State. As the months flew by, he and Angela built the kind of relationship that secures a long future and endures through the trouble spots.

In June of 1938, Curt rearranged his final exam schedule in order to see his radiantly beautiful Angela receive her high school diploma. After the graduation, Angela took only a week off before going down to Columbus, herself, to enroll in summer school.

In June of 1939, it was Angela's turn to sit in the audience with Mr. and Mrs. Bryant as Curt received his bachelor's degree, magna cum laude, from Ohio State. Angela stayed on campus that summer, planning to graduate in three years.

In the fall of 1939, Curt was working on a master's degree in Rehabilitation Science, and Angela was finishing up some sophomore courses, when they received an urgent telephone call from the Millers in Sandusky.

"Angie, can you and Curt get right up here?" Sue pleaded. "It's Miss Foster. I'm afraid she won't last the night."

With her heart heavy, Angela quickly packed an over-

Angela's Crown

night bag and picked up Curt at his rooming house.

"Do you think this beat-up old car will make it, honey?" was all he asked.

They arrived just after dinner, and a nurse showed Angela into Miss Foster's room. Pastor Bob Slayton sat on a chair beside the bed. Miss Foster appeared to be asleep, her hands extended neatly on the sheet drawn up across her chest.

"Miss Foster," said Angela softly, "it's Angie. Can you hear me?" Angela leaned over and gently kissed her forehead. It felt cold.

Miss Foster's head moved, her eyes opened, and she tried to speak. Only a whisper came out, but she seemed to know what was going on.

"Angela," she whispered. "My Angela. My beautiful lady knight has come to take me home."

Tears filled Angela's eyes as the old lady who had made her dreams possible now reached out to her.

"I'm right here, Miss Foster, and I won't leave," said Angela. "Can you rest while I sit with you?"

"No time. No time to rest now, Angie," she whispered. Her eyes strained to focus on Angela's face. "I wanted for a girl—" She gasped for breath. "—for a girl to be what she could be. To learn. To be in charge. To swim. Take my hands, Angela. Take my hands."

Angela squeezed the once-strong hands which were now cold and weak. "I'm here, Miss Foster," she said through her tears. "We'll be together. We'll swim, and . . . I'll be your lady knight."

"Swim, swimming home," Miss Foster whispered. "We finished what we started, you and I. Didn't we, Angie?" She struggled to make herself understood. "We made them see. Ask Pastor Bob . . . to read. . . ."

"If I take the wings of the morning," read Pastor Bob from the 139th Psalm, "and dwell in the uttermost parts of the sea—"

"Oh, swim with me, Angie, swim for your medal," whispered Miss Foster.

"—even there shalt thy hand lead me, and thy right hand shall hold me," he continued reading.

"Hold my hands, take the crown, your incorruptible crown, Angie—" Her breath failed for a moment. "Angie, my lady knight . . . take me home, Angie, home— to God." Her breath stopped.

The room was completely silent for a moment. Angie looked at Pastor Bob.

"I am the Resurrection and the Life, sayeth the Lord," read Pastor Bob, "he that believeth in me, though he were dead, yet shall he live."

Angela's golden hair spread over the sunken chest, now still. Tears streamed down Angie's face. A few minutes later Pastor Bob led Angela out into the hall.

"Is it over?" asked Curt.

"In *this* world," sobbed Angela, "but she wore her crown of gold into the next one."

A week later, in Columbus, Angela and Curt received newspaper clippings about the reading of Miss Foster's will. Amanda Foster had set up a magnificent charitable trust fund and she had named Bob Slayton, David Miller, and Miss Foster's attorney as the trustees. They were given broad discretionary powers to undertake projects which would develop the potential of the destitute and the handicapped. No capital could be spent

Angela's Crown

from the fund, however, until Miss Angela Weber had attained the age of majority, which was twenty-one in Ohio.

At that time, for a period of five years, the directors were to approve any capital project within the scope of the fund that Miss Angela Weber might wish to direct personally, and, should she decline, the fund would become a permanent charitable presence in the Sandusky community.

"What it means, Angie," Sue Miller explained, "is that any time up to the age of 26, you can ask the directors to build a school, or a training center, or a hospital wing, name yourself as the director and operate it for poor, or crippled kids. If you marry, your husband can receive co-director status if the board thinks you picked the right guy."

"I need to hurry up and become 21," said Angela, "and finish up my degree in rehabilitation. I might forget the AAU meet this year and just go for the Olympics."

In the winter of 1940, Angela sat out the AAU Nationals, although she did help some girls around Columbus, who wanted to compete. In the late spring, the Olympic Games scheduled for Japan were called off. Japan had invaded China, Germany had invaded Norway, and the world was in turmoil, the very nightmare that Angela had felt could not happen.

Curt Bryant finished up his master's degree at Ohio State and decided to work at the Ohio State Rehabilitation Center in Columbus for a year while Angela finished up her degree. On February 18, 1941, Angela turned twenty-one, and in June received her bachelor of rehabilitation science degree, magna cum laude, from Ohio State.

One week later, Pastor Bob Slayton struggled to fit more than a thousand people into his little church for a wedding.

Coach David Miller commented on the irony of the situation. "Most coaches try all their lives to find an Olympic champion," he quipped, "and here I am, giving one away."

Angie and Curt enjoyed a deliriously happy wedding trip to Canada, driving all the way to Quebec, with a stopover in Toronto. They called on Mrs. Florence Liddell, wife of the Reverend Eric Liddell, who had taken refuge with their two little girls in Toronto. She was expecting a third child and was terribly worried about her husband. Eric had stayed with his Chinese parish who were suffering persecution from the Japanese.

That fall, the board of directors for the Foster Trust approved the construction of The Crown School, which was to be a residential facility for crippled children, primarily victims of polio and spinal damage. The school would provide forty children with education, therapy, medical attention, all the latest things that healing science could devise.

The building was completed in June of 1942, just as materials were becoming scarce due to war shortages. In the facility there was an apartment for the resident co-directors, Mr. and Mrs. Curt Bryant, a special swimming pool, treatment rooms, classrooms, special dormitories, and counseling rooms.

Mr. Art Glover took charge of the maintenance and his wife, Mary, ran the kitchen and purchased the material for the school.

Angela's Crown

On opening day, Pastor Bob came into the co-directors' office to introduce the first family to Angela and Curt. They were farm people from the Norwalk area. Angela put them at ease right away, and as she talked cheerfully about the care that would be provided for their polio-crippled son, their outlook brightened considerably.

While Angela talked to the parents, Pastor Bob noticed a framed corkboard on the wall behind the co-directors' desks. On it was a large oval composed entirely of swimming, diving, and gymnastics medals, except for a nurse's badge and the Silver Star in the center. All were encircled by the ribbons of two Olympic gold medals which hung just below. Over the board, there was a slogan painted in golden script.

> That Each Child Shall Seek and Wear
> An Incorruptible Crown, A Crown of Purest Gold
> To This End We Dedicate
>   The Crown School

POSTSCRIPT: MAY 1948

Angela Weber Bryant finished brushing her hair, smoothed out her dress, and looked in on the twins. They were in the playroom, busy with little trucks.

"Hi, fellas. How are you doing?" she asked.

"Mommy, Mommy, can we swim with you today?" asked little Pete.

"Mommy has a lady coming in soon," said Angela. "When she leaves, Mommy will take you and Curt swimming. If," she added, "Miss Mary says you have been angels. Well, nearly angels." She smiled proudly at her two handsome little boys.

Angela waved at Mary Zimmerman Glover, whose office was set up with a special window through which she could watch the twins at times. Angela told the boys she would see them soon and hurried down the stairs to the administrative suite in the front of The Crown School. She opened the door marked Co-Directors, and began checking her desk calendar.

Good grief, she thought, *Mrs. Dorothy Ogletree will be here in five minutes.* She now had full responsibility for her crippled grandson since her husband ended up in prison and her son skipped town to escape a bad marriage and bills. *I do feel sorry for her,* Angela thought, *but she's still a pain in the neck!*

Angie's eyes ran on down the schedule. Pick up Curt at the noon train from Cleveland; check the roof repair contract; speech tonight for the Sandusky Athletic Boosters to raise money for the 1948 Olympic team.

Her eyes wandered to the photographs on her desk—Mother in her nurse's uniform, Father in a suit that he seldom wore, and Curt in his army uniform.

Just six months after they had opened The Crown School, with the hard-to-get new staff just barely trained, Curt entered the Medical Service Corps as a First Lieutenant. He specialized in organizing and operating rehabilitation programs for war-wounded. The facilities he operated were used by all the services. Once Curt even had a visit from Lieutenant Adolph Keifer, who was setting up water survival programs for the entire U.S. Navy!

How Angela had struggled to run The Crown School in those early days. The war imposed reductions in staff, materials, transportation, everything, it seemed. But there was no reduction in the number of crippled children with great needs. Fortunately, the Foster Fund trained a nucleus of staff and ran the school well. The Crown School made the headlines in several national magazines and constantly received requests from medical centers to cooperate in research projects.

In May 1944, Captain Bryant got a quick furlough before leaving for Scotland where he was to direct a med-

Postscript: May 1948

ical facility, treating the flood of casualties from the invasion of France.

Angela gloried in the week she could spend with her husband. Then Curt was gone, and Angela was running the school alone, when she discovered that she was pregnant. Her years of athletic training provided her with a remarkably easy pregnancy, and the war news indicated that Curt wouldn't be gone too many more months.

On the afternoon of February 4, 1945, she felt ill. Sue Miller came to stay with her, but Angela talked Sue into going home at bedtime.

"If the kids are anything like they used to be, Sue," laughed Angela, "the principal of Sandusky High School needs his wife home at night."

But after Angela fell asleep, she had a strange dream. In the dream she was swimming a great backstroke race, and in the next lane a man was running. The man wore a track suit, and he reached out to her as he kept sinking.

"Eric," she called. "Eric Liddell, give me your hand." She had never actually seen Eric Liddell but in her dream his face was quite clear.

"You've found your crown, Angie," Eric replied. "You've run the straight race. I'm going now. It's complete surrender to God." Then he was lifted up, as if by unseen hands, running right through the roof and out of her dream.

"Your crown is in your heart, Angie," were the last words she heard.

The next morning Angela went into labor, and Mary drove her to the hospital. Around 2:00 P.M. she delivered twin boys with such remarkable ease that the doctor kidded her about wasting his time.

When little Pete and Curt were four months old, their father returned from World War II.

"Angie," said Curt one night as they were snuggling in bed. "I saw the most beautiful thing a few weeks ago. I saved it to tell you myself."

"What is it, darling?" Angie asked.

"In Edinburgh, just before the German surrender, they got word that Eric Liddell had died, back on February 21, I think. He was in a Japanese internment camp in China, you know. The whole city of Edinburgh turned out to pay honor, and to mourn."

"I already knew," said Angie. "I had a dream, and Eric talked to me as he was leaving. Your sons came the very next day," she said, explaining the whole scene in detail.

They were silent for a little while.

"Angie," Curt said, "you know I'm not a war hero like your father was. All I have is my mustering-out pay, and a couple of service ribbons, and a lot of wounded guys that I tried to help. . . ."

"And a wife who thinks you are the world's greatest champion," said Angela, pulling Curt to her.

There was a tap on the office door, jerking Angela back to 1948. Mrs. Dorothy Ogletree entered.

"Oh, here you are," she said. "Why do I have to come in two days before my grandson? As if I don't have enough to do already!"

"Good morning, Mrs. Ogletree," said Angela. "We have a parents' orientation for all our incoming children. According to the court order, you are little Billy's legal guardian, and so we need to show you the pro-

Postscript: May 1948

gram. Billy's going to get a lot better, but he's going to need all of us on his team!"

"Will he have to be around those—those—well, I hate to say it, Angela, but those horridly deformed-looking children I saw on the playground?" asked Mrs. Ogletree, her face wrinkling.

"The children live here as a family, Mrs. Ogletree," said Angela. "And now it's time for our tour. You must see the whole facility, so you can follow through on the therapy plan after Billy has been here for a year or two."

They walked through The Crown School, while Mrs. Ogletree grumbled and Angela pointed out positive features of each room in the school.

"Dear Angela," said Mrs. Ogletree, "you always were the cheery little optimist. I suppose you enjoy seeing me brought down this way, having to come to you, since I've lost all my money and my husband."

"Not in any way, Mrs. Ogletree," said Angela. "I'm delighted that The Crown School can help little Billy. Many polio victims lead active lives. My husband is an excellent example."

Two eager little boys suddenly emerged from behind a door and charged towards Angela.

"Mommy, Mommy, is this the lady you was seein'?" cried Curt.

"Are we swimmin' wif you and the lady?" asked little Pete.

"Yes, boys, we'll go swimming now," said Angela, gathering up a squirming son in each arm. "Come down to the pool and watch, Mrs. Ogletree. The boys are learning to swim in the shallow end while I do muscle therapy with our students."

"Really, Angela! Your two darling sons? In the therapy pool?" asked Mrs. Ogletree.

"It's always the right time to swim, Mrs. Ogletree—," Angela laughed, "—when you wear a crown in your heart. And you will come to find that out for yourself."

APPENDICES

APPENDIX 1: The 1936 Team, USA Women's Swimming and Diving, the XIth Olympiad at Berlin

1. Alice Bridges (Roche):
   200-meter backstroke, bronze medal; became a swimming instructor

2. Alice Cummings:
   200-meter breaststroke

3. Velma Clancy Dunn:
   Platform diving, silver medal

4. Mavis Ann Freeman:
   4 x 100-meter freestyle relay, bronze medal

5. Marjorie Gestring (Redlick):
   Springboard diving, gold medal; youngest Olympic champion in the history of the Games

6. Bernice Ruth Lapp:
   4 x 100-meter freestyle relay, bronze medal

7. Olive Mary McKean:
   4 x 100-meter freestyle relay, bronze medal

8. Edith Motridge:
   100-meter backstroke, 4th place

9. Mary Lou Petty:
   400-meter freestyle

10. Dorothy Poynton-Hill:
    Platform diving, gold medal; springboard diving, bronze medal; 1932 Los Angeles Games, platform diving, gold medal; 1928 Amsterdam Games, springboard diving, silver medal; TV personality and swim club operator; one of the top woman divers of all time

11. Katherine Louise Rawls (Thompson):
    Springboard diving, silver medal; 4 x 100-meter freestyle relay, bronze medal; 1932 Los Angeles Games, springboard diving, silver medal; 3rd and last Olympic medalist in both swimming and diving; one of the original twenty-five women pilots who ferried planes to the combat zones of World War II with the Air Transport Command

12. Elizabeth Ryan:
    Freestyle events

13. Dorothy Jane Schiller:
    200-meter breaststroke

APPENDIX 2: 1936 Olympics

Events used for this story, as they actually happened

100-meter backstroke:

Gold medal:
   Dina Senff, Netherlands
   Time: 1:18.9 (Olympic Record)

Silver medal:
   Hendrika Mastenbroek, Netherlands (also won gold medals in 100- and 400-meter freestyle, and the

Appendices

       4 x 100-meter freestyle relay)
   Time: 1:19.2

  Bronze medal:
    Alice Bridges, USA
    Time: 1:19.4

Springboard diving:
  Gold medal:
    Marjorie Gestring, USA
    Score: 89.27

  Silver medal:
    Katherine Rawls, USA
    Score: 88.35

  Bronze medal:
    Dorothy Poynton-Hill, USA
    Score: 82.36

NOTE: The substitution of the character Angela Weber in this story as the winner of these two events is fictitious. A total of three women and one man have won medals in both a swimming and a diving event. No one has ever won the gold medal in both categories, nor even competed in both categories since World War II.

APPENDIX 3: Other Olympians

1. Sybil Bauer: USA
100-meter backstroke, 1924 Paris Games, gold medal; died in 1927 of cancer; women's sports pioneer.

2. Ethelda Bleibtrey: USA
100-meter freestyle, 300-meter freestyle, 4 x 100-meter freestyle relay, 1920 Antwerp Games, gold medals; swim coach and famous crusader for women's sports and rights; overcame polio as a young girl.

A LADY, A CHAMPION

3. Gertrude Ederle: USA
   4 x 100 freestyle relay, 1924 Paris Games, gold medal; 100-meter and 400-meter freestyle, 1924 Paris Games, bronze medals; first woman to swim English Channel, 1926, lowering men's record by 17 percent; famous swim teacher and advocate for the handicapped.

4. Ray Ewry: USA
   Standing long jump, broad jump, triple jump, 1900 Paris, 1904 St. Louis, 1906 Athens, 1908 London Games, ten gold medals; overcame boyhood polio; naval architect; designed New York City reservoirs; advocate for the handicapped.

5. Eric Liddell: Great Britain
   400-meter track race, 1924 Paris Games, gold medal (world record); 200-meter track race, 1924 Paris Games, bronze medal; national hero of Scotland and world famous as a Christian missionary and athlete.

6. Lutz Long: Germany
   Long jump, 1936 Berlin Games, silver medal; his act of sportsmanship kept Jesse Owens in the long jump, which Owens then won; he asked Owens to tell his son about Olympic brotherhood sportsmanship; was killed serving in German Army in 1943; Owens stood as best man at the son's wedding.

7. Jack Lovelock: New Zealand
   1500-meter track race, 1936 Berlin Games, gold medal; 1932 Los Angeles Games, 7th; New Zealand's greatest runner; Rhodes scholar, medical doctor, pioneer in runners' physiology; killed, New York City, in accident, 1949.

8. Hendrika (Rie) Mastenbroek: Netherlands
   100-meter freestyle, 400-meter freestyle, 4 x 100-meter freestyle relay, 1936 Berlin Games, gold medals; 100-meter backstroke, 1936 Berlin Games, silver medal; greatest woman swimmer in Netherlands history and one of the world's all-time greats.

Appendices

9. **Jesse Owens: USA**
   100-meter track race, 200-meter track race, 4 x 100-meter relay track race, long jump, 1936 Berlin Games, gold medals; one of the top track athletes in history; awarded the U.S. Presidential Medal of Freedom, the nation's highest civilian honor.

10. **Aileen Riggin: USA**
    Springboard diving, 1920 Antwerp Games, gold medal; springboard diving, 1924 Paris Games, silver medal; 100-meter backstroke, Paris Games, bronze medal; great pioneer in women's swimming and diving; one of only three women in history to win Olympic medals in both swimming and diving.

11. **Helen Wainwright: USA**
    Springboard diving, 1920 Antwerp Games, silver medal; 400-meter freestyle, 1924 Paris Games, bronze medal; one of the three women to win Olympic medals in both swimming and diving; had medals melted down to support World War II effort.

Other Living Books Bestsellers

THE BEST CHRISTMAS PAGEANT EVER by Barbara Robinson. A delightfully wild and funny story about what can happen to a Christmas program when the "horrible Herdman" family of brothers and sisters are miscast in the roles of the Christmas story characters from the Bible. 07-0137 $2.50.

ELIJAH by William H. Stephens. He was a rough-hewn farmer who strolled onto the stage of history to deliver warnings to Ahab the king and to defy Jezebel the queen. A powerful biblical novel you will never forget. 07-4023 $3.95.

THE TOTAL MAN by Dan Benson. A practical guide on how to gain confidence and fulfillment. Covering areas such as budgeting of time, money matters, and marital relationships. 07-7289 $3.50.

HOW TO HAVE ALL THE TIME YOU NEED EVERY DAY by Pat King. Drawing from her own and other women's experiences as well as from the Bible and the research of time experts, Pat has written a warm and personal book for every Christian woman. 07-1529 $3.50.

IT'S INCREDIBLE by Ann Kiemel. "It's incredible" is what some people say when a slim young woman says, "Hi, I'm Ann," and starts talking about love and good and beauty. As Ann tells about a Jesus who can make all the difference in their lives, some call that incredible, and turn away. Others become miracles themselves, agreeing with Ann that it's incredible. 07-1818 $2.50.

THE PEPPERMINT GANG AND THE EVERGEEN CASTLE by Laurie Clifford. A heartwarming story about the growing pains of five children whose hilarious adventures teach them unforgettable lessons about love and forgiveness, life and death. Delightful reading for all ages. 07-0779 $3.50.

JOHN, SON OF THUNDER by Ellen Gunderson Traylor. Travel with John down the desert paths, through the courts of the Holy City, and to the foot of the cross. Journey with him from his luxury as a privileged son of Israel to the bitter hardship of his exile on Patmos. This is a saga of adventure, romance, and discovery—of a man bigger than life—the disciple "whom Jesus loved." 07-1903 $3.95.

WHAT'S IN A NAME? compiled by Linda Francis, John Hartzel, and Al Palmquist. A fascinating name dictionary that features the literal meaning of people's first names, the character quality implied by the name, and an applicable Scripture verse for each name listed. Ideal for expectant parents! 07-7935 $2.95.

Other Living Books Bestsellers

DAVID AND BATHSHEBA by Roberta Kells Dorr. Was Bathsheba an innocent country girl or a scheming adulteress? What was King David really like? Solomon—the wisest man in the world—was to be king, but could he survive his brothers' intrigues? Here is an epic love story which comes radiantly alive through the art of a fine storyteller. 07-0618 $4.50.

TOO MEAN TO DIE by Nick Pirovolos with William Proctor. In this action-packed story, Nick the Greek tells how he grew from a scrappy immigrant boy to a fearless underworld criminal. Finally caught, he was imprisoned. But something remarkable happened and he was set free—truly set free! 07-7283 $3.95.

FOR WOMEN ONLY. This bestseller gives a balanced, entertaining, diversified treatment of all aspects of womanhood. Edited by Evelyn and J. Allan Petersen, founder of Family Concern. 07-0897 $3.95.

FOR MEN ONLY. Edited by J. Allan Petersen, this book gives solid advice on how men can cope with the tremendous pressures they face every day as fathers, husbands, workers. 07-0892 $3.50.

ROCK. What is rock music really doing to you? Bob Larson presents a well-researched and penetrating look at today's rock music and rock performers. What are lyrics really saying? Who are the top performers and what are their life-styles? 07-5686 $2.95.

THE ALCOHOL TRAP by Fred Foster. A successful film executive was about to lose everything—his family's vacation home, his house in New Jersey, his reputation in the film industry, his wife. This is an emotion-packed story of hope and encouragement, offering valuable insights into the troubled world of high pressure living and alcoholism. 07-0078 $2.95.

LET ME BE A WOMAN. Best selling author Elisabeth Elliot (author of *THROUGH GATES OF SPLENDOR*) presents her profound and unique perspective on womanhood. This is a significant book on a continuing controversial subject. 07-2162 $3.50.

WE'RE IN THE ARMY NOW by Imeldia Morris Eller. Five children become their older brother's "army" as they work together to keep their family intact during a time of crisis for their mother. 07-7862 $2.95.

WILD CHILD by Mari Hanes. A heartrending story of a young boy who was abandoned and struggled alone for survival. You will be moved as you read how one woman's love tames this boy who was more animal than human. 07-8224 $2.95.

THE SURGEON'S FAMILY by David Hernandez with Carole Gift Page. This is an incredible three-generation story of a family that has faced danger and death—and has survived. Walking dead-end streets of violence and poverty, often seemingly without hope, the family of David Hernandez has struggled to find a new kind of life. 07-6684 $2.95.

Other Living Books Bestsellers

THE MAN WHO COULD DO NO WRONG by Charles E. Blair with John and Elizabeth Sherrill. He built one of the largest churches in America . . . then he made a mistake. This is the incredible story of Pastor Charles E. Blair, accused of massive fraud. A book "for error-prone people in search of the Christian's secret for handling mistakes." 07-4002 $3.50.

GIVERS, TAKERS AND OTHER KINDS OF LOVERS by Josh McDowell. This book bypasses vague generalities about love and sex and gets right down to basic questions: Whatever happened to sexual freedom? What's true love like? What is your most important sex organ? Do men respond differently than women? If you're looking for straight answers about God's plan for love and sexuality then this book was written for you. 07-1031 $2.50.

MORE THAN A CARPENTER by Josh McDowell. This best selling author thought Christians must be "out of their minds." He put them down. He argued against their faith. But eventually he saw that his arguments wouldn't stand up. In this book, Josh focuses upon the person who changed his life—Jesus Christ. 07-4552 $2.50.

HIND'S FEET ON HIGH PLACES by Hannah Hurnard. A classic allegory which has sold more than a million copies! 07-1429 $3.50.

THE CATCH ME KILLER by Bob Erler with John Souter. Golden gloves, black belt, green beret, silver badge. Supercop Bob Erler had earned the colors of manhood. Now can he survive prison life? An incredible true story of forgiveness and hope. 07-0214 $3.50.

WHAT WIVES WISH THEIR HUSBANDS KNEW ABOUT WOMEN by Dr. James Dobson. By the best selling author of *DARE TO DISCIPLINE* and *THE STRONG-WILLED CHILD*, here's a vital book that speaks to the unique emotional needs and aspirations of today's woman. An immensely practical, interesting guide. 07-7896 $2.95.

PONTIUS PILATE by Dr. Paul Maier. This fascinating novel is about one of the most famous Romans in history—the man who declared Jesus innocent but who nevertheless sent him to the cross. This powerful biblical novel gives you a unique insight into the life and death of Jesus. 07-4852 $3.95.

LIFE IS TREMENDOUS by Charlie Jones. Believing that enthusiasm makes the difference, Jones shows how anyone can be happy, involved, relevant, productive, healthy, and secure in the midst of a high-pressure, commercialized, automated society. 07-2184 $2.50.

HOW TO BE HAPPY THOUGH MARRIED by Dr. Tim LaHaye. One of America's most successful marriage counselors gives practical, proven advice for marital happiness. 07-1499 $2.95.

The books listed are available at your bookstore. If unavailable, send check with order to cover retail price plus 10% for postage and handling to:

Tyndale House Publishers, Inc.
Box 80
Wheaton, Illinois 60189

Prices and availability subject to change without notice. Allow 4–6 weeks for delivery.